Shadows of Timber Creek

S.J. Chaynie

Contents

"The only thing we have to fear, is fear itself."
-Franklin D. Roosevelt

To Callie. You're my freaking hero.

READER NOTE

This book contains sensitive topics they may be triggering to some readers. Please be aware the heroine is hearing impaired, and there are also elements of domestic violence displayed.

PROLOGUE

Greyson

I sit with my head in my hands. My elbows planted on the cold tabletop. I never expected to be in this room. Never expected for things to turn out the way they did. The grinding sound of the thirty-year-old hinges has me lifting my head. My heavy eyes snag on the pair of shoes that enter the room. I let out a solid breath before I lean back in my chair.

Slowly, I meet the eyes of my brother. A man I would trust with my life. He braces his palms on the table across from me, head bowed, and shoulders bunched. Tension rolls off of him in waves, wrapping tight around my throat.

"It's not looking good, Grey." His hoarse voice reaches my ears and I clam up. Sweat breaks out on the back of my neck and my stomach rolls with nausea.

"The evidence is stacked against you." He lifts his head. "What the fuck happened?"

I shake my head, running a hand over my face. "It's not what it looks like, East."

He stands tall, his hands hanging by his side. "I can only do so much. It's too close to home. The sheriff will step in. Then it's out of our hands."

I nod. "I understand."

"I don't think you do, brother." He pauses. "They're gonna charge you."

I clench my fists. "I was protecting her."

Just like I promised.

"It doesn't matter. What matters is what they can prove." His eyes penetrate me with a pity I hate. "And right now, the evidence proves it was you."

CHAPTER 1

Greyson

Two weeks earlier.

I finish my last rep with a feral grunt. Sweat drips from my forehead as I place the bar on the rack with unnecessary force. My workouts are probably the only thing keeping me sane at this point. It's off season. You would think the media vultures would have better things to do, but unfortunately, a scandal involving me and my good for nothing father is what's taking the leader board right now.

Which is the reason I have four missed calls from my Coach, one from Mavery, the head of PR for the team, and my brother.

Yanking my shirt off, I toss it in the over flowing bin of laundry and shut off the music. I'm not ready to face the cluster fuck that is my life yet.

For now, I'll take a hot shower and drink until I pass out. Like I have for the last week.

My phone rings and I reluctantly answer. Coach Rusk is annoyingly persistent and he ain't gonna let up.

"Coach," I answer flatly.

"Greyson. Avoiding me?" He questions.

"Maybe," I answer honestly.

"I know it's a shit show right now, and I know you got some family stuff going on, but we gotta get a handle on this."

I tilt my head back, sighing at the fact I even have to deal with this. "I thought that's what Mavery is for."

"It is and she's saving your ass right now," he grits out.

"Yeah, leaking pictures of me and Anna Leslie like we're already three steps down the aisle," I scoff. "It was a few charity events and I wouldn't touch her with a ten foot pole, so I sure as shit am not letting her anywhere near my dick."

"Look, it's better people are speculating about your love life rather than the fact you beat your father half to death in a very public place," he counters.

My father. Anger soars through me at the thought. He deserves every punch I landed. He deserves it for destroying my mother and the damage he did to my brother. What kind of man pays his mistress whose half his age to say the child they created was actually his own son's? For four fucking years.

"They better be glad I left him alive," I seethe.

"I need you out of prison. We gotta win the bowl this year." He chuckles.

"I'm fine. I just need to get my head right." I walk into my bathroom and flip on the faucet to the shower.

"Good. In the meantime, lay low and behave."

"Yes sir." I hang up, tossing my cell onto the countertop before I slide down my shorts.

Just as I'm stepping onto the cold tile, my phone rings again.

Easton.

If I have a soft spot for anyone right now, it's him.

Swiping the screen, I pick up. "Brother."

"Hey man."

"What's up?" I pinch the bridge of nose, not looking forward to another conversation regarding our family matters.

"Nothing much, just calling to check in."

His tone is off, and it immediately sends me on alert. "East."

I'm not sure if my voice holds a question or a warning. I'm standing buck naked, and he wants to beat around the bush.

"You talked to Adam?" He asks.

"Nah. Why?"

I'm not sure why he's asking about Adam. Adam Harper has been my best friend since third grade. He's a police officer, along with my brother and I can't deny that sometimes I'm just waiting for *that* call. The call no one wants to get about someone they've spent decades of their life with.

"What's wrong?" I finally ask.

"Nothing is wrong...." He clears his throat. "It's Tilly."

Ice. Cold, soul crushing ice fills my veins at the mention of her name. My best friend's little sister.

I swallow. "What about her?"

"Grey......she's." He pauses and sighs. "She's engaged."

I freeze. All I can do is stare absently back at myself in the mirror. All I can focus on is the light layer of steam gravitating over my reflection. The sound of the water pounding against the floor of the shower.

"Grey? You there?" He asks.

"What the fuck do you mean, engaged?" I bark out.

"Her boyfriend proposed last night."

"Boyfriend? What boyfriend?"

I was aware she had gone on some dates, and she had company the last time we had seen each other. I had showed up unannounced, and had a rude awakening, but how in the world did she go from a few dates to engaged?

"I'm as shocked as you are. She's only been dating him a couple of months."

My limbs regain function and I'm on the move to the bedroom, still naked as the day I was born while I reach for my suitcase inside the closet.

"What are you doing?" He asks.

"Packing."

"Fuck..." he mutters.

"I'll be there tomorrow morning." I storm back to the bathroom. "She's not marrying him."

"Greyson, you can't just...." he starts.

"Can't what Easton? If this was Elle? What would you do?"

There's another silence on his end before he answers. "I'd already be on a plane."

"That's what I thought." I hang up and flip open my suitcase. This isn't how it ends. *It can't be.*

CHAPTER 2

Tilly

There's never been a time that silence was awkward for me. I was born deaf. My world was silent for the first years of my life. Profound in one ear and severe to profound in the other. There's a bunch of medical terms and words like "frequency" involved, but I prefer to call a spade a spade. *I'm deaf.* I can't hear shit. Not without help. I'm fortunate to have a pair of fancy hearing aids that do the work for me. As much as I love being able to hear. To listen. Sometimes the silence is my safe haven. But right now, this silence is about to bring up the contents of my dinner.

"These cookies are good. Moist." Bekka, my best friend tries to evaporate the awkward vibe in the room but fails miserably because there probably isn't another word more cringe worthy than *moist.*

She scrunches her nose, and glances at my twin sister, Camille, who's studying me with light blue eyes that are almost identical to mine. Elle, who's seated next to my sister appears to be busting at the seams.

Because she was never one to keep her mouth shut, she finally slings back the last of her wine. "So, are we just going to ignore the massive elephant in the room?"

I close my eyes and tilt my head back. I knew this was coming. I mean, I literally got engaged less than twenty four hours ago. To a man I've known for approximately three months. I've been known to be somewhat impulsive. My father, who happens to be the Timber Creek Police captain has always said I'd be the child that would end up on his police scanner. I'd be the one to break the law and have a smile while doing it. I was no where near a criminal. He was just being dramatic. He and my brother had always been over the top. I didn't break the *law*. I just broke the rules.

I wasn't defiant per se, but if I wanted to prove a point, I did. I hated that my rules were always different from everyone else's and that tended to get me into trouble. My need for validation was just as strong as my temper, so those two didn't mix well when one conflicted with the other.

I lift my hand, examining the diamond ring on my finger that's entirely too big. Blaine McKnight had been pursuing me since I met him at a New Years Eve party I attended with one of my coworkers. He was charming. Had a great smile and any woman with eyes could tell he was handsome. Sandy blonde hair and brown eyes. He worked for his father's private law firm in the city where he lives in a snazzy condo. It took a few times of him calling for me to finally agree to a date. I didn't date much. Most of the men in Timber Creek I'd known my entire life and the others I've met socially never lasted past the *by the way I'm deaf* stage.

ASL was my first language, but when I got my hearing aids, my speech improved. It took lots of tears, speech therapy, and pep talks, but now I can be a chatter box in the right setting. Confidence in my voice is something I still struggle with and in large groups or public settings I often sign.

The uncomfortable conversation about my hearing is usually when they tuck their tail and run. Which is fine. I don't want a man who doesn't accept me for who I am. Me and the hearing aids are a package deal and if a man can't accept that, he can check himself at the door. But Blaine has been understanding. He's really not even mentioned it after the initial conversation.

"It's only been what? A few months?" Elle asks.

"We've been official for a month," I state.

I inwardly cringe. It sounds awful when I actually say it out loud.

"We've literally only met him twice." Camille huffs and crosses her legs.

"He has a very demanding job, Cami," I defend.

Which he does. He works a lot. But that benefits me because I'm busy with teaching my ASL classes at the Timber Creek Center. We see each other a couple of times a week. He calls when he says and he sends flowers on Friday's. *He's safe.* I know that's not typically what you say when you think of the person you will spend the rest of your life with, but my circumstances are different. I don't have a line half way down Main Street waiting to take a shot with Tilly Harper. The only man I have ever loved didn't give a damn about me. I've spent too many years angry. Too many years waiting for him to see me. So, I've moved on. I have someone who's making an effort and at twenty-five years old, I need to start thinking about my future. *Family.*

"It just seems sudden, Tills," Cami expresses.

"You and Jace only knew each other for a month." I lift a brow.

Her lips thin into a line and she shifts on the couch.

"Are you pregnant?" Elle leans forward, her eagerness evident like I'm about to spill some grade A tea.

"No. I'm not pregnant." I roll my eyes.

"This isn't about...." my sister trails off.

My eyes narrow and Bekka clears her throat. She knows this may lead down a dangerous avenue.

Don't say it. *I swear I'll lose my shit.*

Camille's eyes soften and she gives me a look only twins can comprehend. The look that says *I know you.*

"Is this a reaction to Greyson?" She asks.

And that's my que to shut this conversation down. I push to stand on my fuzzy socks.

It's late. I have early classes in the morning. I sign because now I'm pissed.

She visibly shrinks back onto the couch, and I hate that I'm being a bitch. But this has nothing to do with Greyson Roy. Nothing to do with the fact he's been pictured on every social media site with a beautiful woman clinging to his stout body. It has nothing to do with the article that leaked information from a direct source that says the "couple" are getting serious.

It has nothing to do with my brother's best friend.

Nothing to do with what happened a month ago.

So why can't I breathe anytime someone says his name?

CHAPTER 3

Greyson

My feet hit the ground as I climb out of my truck. I didn't even bother with my suitcase. As much as I love my brother, he, Elle, and June are a family now, living in what was my house, but I deeded it over to him a few weeks ago. I spend ninety percent of my time in San Antonio, so it felt right. He deserved it. I had enough money to buy any house I wanted. Multiple actually, but that wasn't really my style. Sure, I had an impressive salary. My contract with the Eagles is more than fair. I prefer to be smart with my money. I have investments and some charities I work with. At the end of the day, I don't play football for the money. I do it for the love of the sport. The money is just a bonus and material shit doesn't mean anything to me. So, I figured I'd stay at my childhood home while I'm here. Dad moved out and mom has been juggling the life of being a new divorcee. I figured she could use the company.

I could hear the familiar music as soon as I hit the porch. I recognized my niece's...or *half-sister's* .... favorite movie. I'm still wrapping my brain around it. I've been "Unky Grey" for the first four years of her life and we agreed it should stay that way. Regardless of who her DNA belongs to. Easton is her dad and Elle is her mom. Plain and simple.

I knock twice before I'm yanking open the door. June is standing on the couch, dressed in her sparkling blue Elsa gown, reciting every word coming from the television. She spins around and her grin spreads as she launches herself off the couch and sprints to meet me in the foyer.

"Unky Grey!!!!" She squeals.

I caught her midair, and her left foot barely missed my balls.

I swear kids have no respect for the male anatomy.

"Hey sweet pea." I drop a kiss on her brown curls and set her on her bare feet.

"Like my toes?" She wiggles her bright pink toenails.

"I love them."

"Can I paint yours?" She asks.

I wince.

"Maybe later. Where's your dad?" I brace my hands on my hips and glance into the kitchen.

The door to the back porch opens and Easton walks in, followed by Elle. He was in his uniform. He must be on duty today.

"Hey man." He nods.

His eyes squint. Like he's sizing me up. Making sure I'm not about to blow a gasket.

"Hey Grey." Elle sits her coat down on the table and takes a few steps over to give me a hug. "I didn't know you were coming into town." She smiles, but she has a gleam in her eye.

I wasn't sure if Easton opened his mouth or if she had a hunch. Elle had a front row seat to a heated moment between Tilly and I at the charity auction last month. She had asked about it later, and I blew her off. I wasn't ready to talk about it at the time.

"Yeah. It was a last minute thing." I clear my throat.

"Hmmm," she hums before moving over to June.

She leans down to whisper in her ear. June takes off up the stairs and I follow my brother and Elle into the kitchen. I sit down on a bar stool and run a hand through my hair. I had never really voiced my relationship or my feelings towards my best friend's sister. That's what she was to me for years. A kid. But when she got older, things shifted. When their mother died and she shut down, Adam came to me for help. It's something I never saw coming and something I damn sure can't explain.

Easton somehow *just* knew. I never had to tell him details. The only thing I ever asked of him was to take care of her while I was gone.

Which is code for I love her, but I can't be here. Not now.

But time wasn't a luxury at the moment. I was kicking my own ass. I know it's what was best. I know she hates me for it.

I was gone for too long.

And just like on the field, the clock was ticking, and I wasn't about to let some fucker in a sweater vest get my girl. So, I didn't rely on formalities or feeling out the situation. I look straight at Elle. She's been close with Tilly for years and she was a straight shooter. No bullshit.

She locks eyes with me, and I ask the question that has my insides burning.

"Is she in love with him?"

She glances at Easton who leans back against the counter before she looks back at me. "It's not really my place to say how she feels."

"Eloise." My tone was sharp. I didn't need vague. I needed answers. Because this matters.

"I've only been around them together a few times." She chews on her lip before she tilts her head.

"You know her, Elle. So, I'm gonna ask again. Is she in love with him?" I hold my breath.

Fuck, I hate this.

She's silent for a moment before she shakes her head. "No. Grey." She reaches out and places her hand on my forearm. "I don't think she's in love with him."

The relief I feel is overwhelming.

"She's reacting." She squeezes my arm. "I don't know what happened between you two in the past or what the story is, but all I will say is this." She steps back. "Don't play with her heart, Greyson. Either make it yours, or let it go."

Let it go? I haven't let go in seven years. Why would I do it now?

CHAPTER 4

Tilly

"Knock knock."

I peer up from my computer to see Lucy in my doorway. Lucy is one of my former students, who turned into a volunteer, who's now an employee and I would consider a good friend. Her father had lost his hearing and they both had to learn ASL to communicate. We formed a pretty tight bond, and the girl makes my job a heck of a lot easier.

"Patty called. Tara has the flu so she can't make her class today." She enters the room, my favorite coffee in hand.

"Aw. Poor thing." I bring my hand to my mouse, clearing out the slot for Tara from my schedule.

That gives me an hour to hopefully get this office somewhat organized. It's a mad house in here.

"Yeah. Apparently, it's going around." She smiles, extending the delicious cup of caffeine. "So careful on the tonsil hockey with your new fiancé."

I laugh, but it's not hearty and light. It's nervous as I take the cup from her hand. "I guess everyone's heard about it by now?"

"It's Timber Creek, Tilly." She grips the file folder that's placed under her arm.

"Yeah." I use my fingers to gently touch the platinum band.

"Congratulations. Have y'all set a date?" She asks.

"No." I let out a breath. "It was kind of...a fast unfolding of events."

"It's not like you have to get married tomorrow," she points out.

"True." I take a sip, closing my eyes as the flavors hit my tongue.

"Here." She hands me the file. "This month's volunteer list. The details of all three outreach program days, your new student requests, and as always lasts month's achieved goal spreadsheet."

I sigh and take the folder. "Have I mentioned you're the best?"

"I mean, it doesn't hurt to hear it every day." She flicks her red hair with a lift of her shoulder.

"You're the best Luce." I raise my cup to her.

She chuckles. "It's my job to take care of you, Tills. Now get to work and stop fantasizing about Blaine's tight ass."

I snort out a laugh as she saunters off.

His ass is nice. Not as nice as....

I shake my head, ridding myself of the heinous thought. I'm engaged. I'm happy. I'm finally letting myself be happy.

I shuffle a few papers, moving them to another stack that I should throw away, but I have a weird attachment to paper. I hate throwing anything away. Which is why my office looks like an F5 tornado did some serious damage. I'll own my weaknesses. I'm not tidy. I'm messy and typically procrastinating, but I take this job seriously and it's my passion, so last minute or not, I give it my all. I usually fly by the seat of pants, which explains the impromptu engagement that's got everyone I've seen this morning either giving me questioning glances or overly enthusiastic well wishes.

My fingers reach up, rubbing over my temples as my phone that's under a stack of papers chirps.

Bekka: Heads up. He's in town.

I read the text and my stomach bottoms out. I'm not sure what the feeling is exactly. Nerves. Anger. Excitement. Dread. Hate.

I don't even get to analyze it because there's another knock at my door.

"Lucy……" I begin.

As if the universe decided to shift. The atmosphere changes, and a feeling I'm all too familiar with flanks the room.

Lucy isn't who takes up the entire doorway to my office. No. I don't even have to spin around in my chair to know who stands in that doorway. The fresh layer of goosebumps tell me all on their own. But because I'm a professional, at work, I slowly turn, facing the open doorway.

My eyes drink in the six-foot five man that lingers in the open space. I try to keep my face neutral. I was in no way happy to see him, but I didn't want to give off the vibe that he affects me. *Because he doesn't. Not anymore.* I left my school girl crush on my brother's best friend behind years ago. *At least that's what I tell myself.*

He moves his broad shoulders and steps in, placing those piercing golden eyes on mine. My fingers clench the wooden hand rests of my chair as I force a blank expression. I'm still angry at him. Still boiling from our last interaction.

Greyson, I sign without speaking, hopefully giving off the *don't test me vibes.*

But the infuriatingly gorgeous tight end just smirks and rasps out. "Hey Rosie." While simultaneously moving his hands to sign it as well.

Butterflies exploded at the nickname, and I grit my teeth. I loathed him. Couldn't even bare to look at him without rage and lust battling for a permanent position in my bones like it was World War three. But I knew better. Greyson Roy may be God's gift to football, but to me, he was nothing but a walking heartache. A playboy. And I refuse to get my heart broken again.

CHAPTER 5

Greyson

She was so fucking pretty.

I've escorted super models, the occasional actress, and women of all types and tax brackets. The one's society claims as "beautiful." Not one of them compares to the woman that currently sits behind her desk, doing her damndest to keep her emotions in check. I learned early on how stubborn this woman was, but that stubbornness is what has set her apart. It's what has pushed her through every challenge she's faced since birth. *And that's the sexiest thing in the world to me.*

I take a seat in the leather chair across from her, carefully assessing every feature. Like she should look different somehow. I mean, she *is* now an engaged woman. A woman who is promised to someone else. But that's not what I saw. I saw Tilly Harper for what she always was.

Mine.

Can I help you? She signs, before folding her hands on her desk like this was any other consultation.

I lift a brow. *Do I need a reason to stop by?* I sign back.

She straightens her shoulders. *Actually yes. If you are here about volunteering, you need to see Dixie. I'm busy.*

She motions her hand around the room. The room that was the perfect reflection of who she was.

A beautiful mess.

I hike my ankle up onto my knee. I didn't respond. I just let my gaze continue to document the things that were the same and the things that had changed. She squirms in her seat under my stare and I doubt she even realizes she's anxiously spinning the ring on her left hand.

His fucking ring.

I move my attention back to her eyes and bring my hands up. *Congratulations.*

She swallows thickly and just like she always did when she was nervous, her fingers reach up to pick at her bottom lip after she signs, *thank you.*

I lean up from the chair, planting both feet on the ground as I reach across the desk. My hand catches her wrist, and her eyes widen. I slowly lower her hand from her lips, like I had done a million times and a light gasp escapes her at the contact.

I couldn't help but glance down at the diamond. It was flashy. Nothing like my Rosie at all. I ran my finger over her knuckle, letting the feel of her skin give me the fix I had been craving for weeks. A few seconds of silence linger between us when her phone rings. The screen lights up with the name *Blaine.*

Her eyes flicker up to mine. I keep a hold of her hand, waiting to see what move she would make. Silently daring her to just let it ring.

On the third ring she tugs her hand away. *I need to take this,* she signs, fingers still graceful as ever.

I nod. "Don't mind me," I say aloud and settle back in my seat.

She huffs out a sigh as she stands, giving me her back as she answers the phone.

"Hello." Her voice is even.

I let my chin rest against my hand as I rake my eyes down her body. The same one had I touched not too long ago.

"No. That's fine." She clears her throat. "I miss you too."

I've been sacked by three hundred pounds of pure muscle countless times and none of those inflicted pain like hearing her say those words.

Did she really mean it?

Was it a natural response?

Did she miss me?

"Yeah. This weekend is still good." She drops her hand down and moves a few papers.

"Alright."

Her hand goes back to her plump lip.

"Ok. You too, bye," she rushes out before hanging up the phone.

She keeps her back to me for a moment. If I know her, she's resetting. Gathering her wits.

She spins around and faces me.

I have class. You need to leave. She moves her hands effortlessly.

It almost made me laugh. She knows I love her voice so she's not giving it to me. Even though I just heard her speak, it wasn't *for* me.

Punishment I'm assuming.

She's going to play it like that? Honestly, I expected nothing less.

"Meet me later?" I ask.

She snorts out a laugh. *No.*

"Why not?"

I'm engaged.

"What's your point?"

Her eyes narrow. *It's inappropriate.*

I smirk and push to my feet. Casually I walk to the door, letting her think she's won this round. When I make it just outside, I turn back. "Nah, inappropriate would be letting me kiss you senseless while your *fiancé* was upstairs. In *your* bed."

Her jaw drops and I knock my knuckles against the door before I saunter off.

I came to play, because Tilly Harper.... she was a whole different ball game.

CHAPTER 6

Greyson

Last month.

The bottle in my hand is almost empty. I wasn't completely numb, but the pain and raging anger had subsided just enough I felt mellow. I knew the only thing that would bring me out of this funk. Out of my self-destruction.

Her.

It may have been years since I've let myself get close to her. Allow myself anything more than a few minutes of conversation. Not much contact. That would just counteract everything. But tonight was different. I got some news that alters the course of my life.

I've only had one thing that was constant. One thing that I consistently loved more than football and since I was in town for the annual charity auction, there was no holding me back. Not in this state.

My hand reaches, up, knocking on Tilly Harper's front door.

It was late. Sometime after two AM. I wasn't exactly sure because I had cut off my phone when I got into town tonight.

A few minutes pass before the door opens. I was surprised because I knew she didn't sleep with her hearing aids in and chances she heard me were slim.

My hands are braced against the door frame and my head that was hanging lifts at her voice.

"Greyson?"

God, she was beautiful. Big blue eyes. Golden hair. Those pouty lips and that dainty nose that turned up just a little at the end. She was just as gorgeous as she was seven years ago. When I broke her heart because at the time, it's what I had to do.

But now......

My gaze holds hers as the words slip out of my mouth. "I need you."

Her eyes widen and her lips part as I take a step in, backing her up inside the foyer.

"Grey," she croaks out.

I shut the door behind me as her hands lift to plant on my chest.

She was so small compared to me. But even so, she fit right against me like she was made to be there. I lift my palm, cupping her jaw before my thumb ran across her bottom lip.

"I..." she starts.

"I miss you," I mutter before my own lips are capturing hers.

The hands on my chest ball into fists and she clenches onto my shirt. My mouth opens, tongue swiping out to taste the sweetness I haven't had the privilege to devour in seven long years. Both of my hands cup her face as I deepen the kiss. She kisses me back, but it's angry. Resentful. Like she hates me for doing this to her. For waiting so long.

My teeth graze across her lip and I suck hard, pulling out a desperate whimper.

"Baby.... I'm sorry. I'm so sorry," I murmur against her.

Like a bolt of lightning, her hands unclench, and she shoves me back. I stumble a few steps, righting myself as I meet her tear filled eyes.

I can't. She signs.

My heart thunders against my rib cage as I take a step toward her. Then I hear it. A voice from upstairs.

"Tilly? Babe you down there?"

She froze and so did my fucking heart.

"Yeah." She briefly closes her eyes. "I was just getting a drink. Be up in a minute," she calls out.

She was with someone. He was here. In her bed.

I move one more step, but she holds up her hand.

She shakes her head, blonde hair swiping across her shoulders.

I need you to leave she signs with unsteady hands.

She blinks away unshed tears and quickly opens the door. I had waited seven years for that kiss and even though I left, just like she asked me to.....I knew this wasn't even close to over.

CHAPTER 7

Tilly

I spend the remainder of my day distracted. He had some nerve. Showing up at my office.

Showing up at my *house at two in the morning.* Such a *Greyson* thing to do.

The evening air is cool and thin as I march to my car and slam my door. It had been a long day, and I could finally breathe as I rest my head against the fabric of my seat.

I remember that night like it was yesterday. I can still *taste* the whiskey. Feel his hands. Then I remember what kind of person that makes me. I was caught off guard. It was late. I was half asleep.

I let out a deep and guilty sigh. I could sit here and make up excuse after excuse, but none of them would be valid. The fact was the man I'd spent the better part of my teen years and an unhealthy amount of time into adulthood in love with, showed up at my door and told me he needed me. *Missed me.* Then his lips hit mine. I should have pushed him away immediately. I should have been enraged.

But the truth is, I wasn't. And *that* is what makes me furious. That he holds that much power over me. That he could just waltz in whenever *he* felt like it and turn my world upside down.

Nothing jolted me back into reality like having my overnight guest interrupt the moment. The moment that should have never even happened. It doesn't matter that Blaine and I hadn't officially labeled our relationship. We weren't exclusive, but it still made me the scum of the earth. He hadn't even meant to stay over. We had been watching a movie and we fell asleep.

A rapid tap on my window causes me to shriek and I rest my hand on my chest when I see Bryson's face smiling back at me.

I quickly roll down the window and he chuckles. "Forget something?" He holds up my cell phone.

I was in such a fluster to get out of there I must have left it on my desk. "What would I do without you?" I say as I pluck my phone from his fingers.

"I'd hate to find out." He winks.

I give him a smile and toss my phone in my purse. Bryson and I had a brief dating period. I wouldn't even call it dating. We went out twice and that was before we worked together. He's a sweet guy, but we just didn't mesh. Thank God we've been able to remain friends. He's our IT man and can work wonders on anything electronic. He's excellent at his job.

"Have a good night." He waves before walking to his truck, leaving the parking lot.

By the time I make it home I've already decided to get wine drunk and watch anything that doesn't revolve around football or hopeless romance. Maybe a good horror film will do the trick.

I just need to take a moment. Redirect. Get my life back on track. Nothing should change now that he's here.

Funny, even as I think the thought, deep down I already know. *Everything has changed.*

I was teetering towards the perfect level of wine drunk when there was a pounding on my door. Setting down my half empty glass, I stand from the couch and make my way across the chilly wood floors. I coo a few words to Nelson, my hedgehog that wiggles his little nose, then buries himself in the warm corner of his cage. Government name, Quilly Nelson, was close to drowning in a drainage ditch this summer and I just happen to pass by on my morning run. What kind of human would I be if I left him there suffering?

Now he's spoiled rotten and listens to me rant and rave when I have the slightest inconvenience. I've deemed him my official support animal. *Poor guy.*

Another pound sounds through the cabin and I laugh because I can tell by the rhythm it's Bekka.

I open the door with a wave of my hand to usher her in. She barrels through without a glance in my direction.

"I just thought I'd…" she trails off when she looks at the wine bottle and *Scream* playing on the tv. "Oh." She spins around. "You saw him, huh?"

Am I that predictable?

I roll my eyes and collapse back down on the couch. "Is it that obvious?"

Bekka is the only soul I have verbally confessed my feelings to about Greyson. It's embarrassing enough the way I apparently misread our relationship……friendship….whatever it was. I would die of mortification if everyone knew how heartbroken I was when he couldn't have cared less. I mean why would he? I was a seventeen-year-old girl, and he was practically famous, heading out to start his NFL career. Which despite everything, I'm proud of. It's not that I didn't want him to chase that dream…I wasn't naive. But the way he went about it what something I just didn't know if I could forgive.

Her eyes widen and she perches on the arm of the couch, swiping a curly piece of black hair from her face. "What did he say?"

"Oh nothing. Just being his typical self. Cocky and overstepping," I scoff.

"Did he address the ring?" She smirks.

"He did. Said congratulations then asked me to meet up with him later." I throw my hands up. "Like we're just best friends."

"Yeah, that's probably not a good idea considering he was rounding second base while Blaine was literally on the floor above you."

I groan. "Bekka."

She shrugs. "What? You're the one that leaked that drama. I didn't even ask."

She's right. I was panicking. I felt dirty, but simultaneously buzzing with a feeling I hadn't felt in years, and I didn't know what to do. When I saw Greyson the next day at the charity auction, after I got past the initial shock of what happened, I was fed up. Some angry words were exchanged and I even slapped him across the face. Hard.

I close my eyes and replay his words in my head. The ones that ignited a raging fire I couldn't contain.

Look me in the eye. Look me in the eye and tell me that when I had you in my arms you didn't forget he even existed.

It wasn't fair. I spent seven years trying to forget Greyson Roy and in a split second I forgot about Blaine McKnight. The man I'm supposed to be committing my life to.

I toss myself on my back and fling my elbow over my face. "I hate him, Bekka."

I hear her snort. "No, you don't." I feel movement, then she's pulling my arm from my face. "You love him. *That's* what you hate."

"I do not. I'm getting married," I defend.

"You can't bullshit a bullshitter, Tills." She taps my nose. "With that said, I'm your best friend. So, if we're pretending to hate Greyson Roy." She picks up my wine glass and takes an audible gulp. "I'll get my hate face on."

"You do realize he's my brother's other favorite person besides you, right?" I cock a brow.

She laughs. "Yes. I'm aware. But you know the rule."

I grin. "To the moon?"

She smiles and hands me the bottle. "To the moon."

To the moon and back. Now that's friendship.

CHAPTER 8

Greyson

I'm sitting at the kitchen table, scrolling through a bunch of bull-shit the media has sprouted out in the last twenty-four hours. One headline reads,

Roy leaves Texas. Rehab?

Another reads.

Is Greyson Roy spiraling?

And the cherry on top reads,

NFL star Greyson Roy and model Anna Leslie in love.

I toss my phone down and groan. This wasn't part of the bargain that I enjoyed. I enjoyed the field. The win. My team mates. Speaking of....

I snatch up my phone and hit Krew's contact. He's one of my closest friends next to Adam, and our quarterback. He doesn't even know I left. Well, I guess he might if he's opened Twitter this morning.

"Sleep late, sweetheart?" I mock when he answers.

"Fuck off Roy. I've been up since four."

"Already on the second workout of the day?" I ask.

"Yep. First one is at four. Conditioning at eight. You know the drill." I can hear him open a door and slam it.

There isn't a man I know more committed than Krew. He works his ass off. Frankly I'm not sure if it's just his love of the game or it's how he battles his demons. Either way he's a fucking force on the field.

"Copy that." I glance over at the empty kitchen.

"You up for a run?" He asks.

"I'm not at the house. I came back home last night," I admit.

I can hear him gulp something down. "Is this a see the family visit or is this about her?"

"Her?" I probe, acting as if I have no clue who he's referring to.

"Your girl." I can hear his smirk through the phone. *Dick.*

"She's not *my girl,* " I grit out.

Not publicly anyway. *Yet.*

"I spent the last five years living next door to you, Greyson. Despite your grumpy ass, you get rather chatty when you're drunk."

"We've been through this." I run my hand across the smooth slate counter top. "She's Adam's sister."

"I guess it's good thing you're in love with Anna Leslie, yeah?"

I scoff out a laugh. "Yeah. In her dreams."

He chuckles.

"I could kill Mavery for that shit," I grumble.

"She's just doing her job."

Now it's my turn to smirk. "Sorry. Didn't mean to rag on *your girl.* "

"She's not," he bites out.

"You sure? I saw Kincaid getting really friendly with her last week."

"Kincaid is a fucking pig and we're all bound to the no fraternizing policy."

"Right. Especially you, huh?" I smile.

"Someone's on the other line. Catch you later," he mumbles.

"Later." I chuckle.

It's nice to know I'm not the only one obsessed with someone I can't have.

For the time being anyway. I have a plan. That plan may wreck my friendship, but I've spent too many years at a distance. I know what I want, and I'll never forgive myself if I don't try.

Three hours later I had a meeting with my doctor via zoom. He wasn't happy that I missed our appointment in person, but I had more important things on the agenda.

"Greyson," Dr. Houser greets.

"Doc." I nod.

I'm still in my spot at the bar, laptop in place.

"I'm glad we could still meet. I think it's important we discuss the scan results in more depth."

"Alight." I shift in my seat.

It started with some dizzy spells, which is normal after a concussion. But when one concussion turned into four and the dizzy spells became more frequent, I started to pay attention. Then when I had my first blackout, waking up confused and agitated, I knew something wasn't right. I fought it for a while. No one wants to admit their mind isn't right, but after I did some research, I made the call.

"Now you know from our last appointment we did scans and looked at all of your symptoms and even ran blood work." He scrolls on his iPad. "I'm emailing all of this to you."

He sighs and adjusts the glasses on his nose. "Greyson I'm going to be straight with you. I've treated a lot of athletes. A lot of football players that have had brain injuries. I'm not diagnosing you, because CTE can't be diagnosed unfortunately until an autopsy is performed.

"Geez, Doc," I scoff.

"I'm not saying you're dying. You are far from that," he counters.

"So, what are you saying?" I ask.

"I'm saying retirement is looking like your next step. You've had too many injuries and if you keep it up at this rate, I wouldn't be surprised if the end result is CTE. Your symptoms are minimal right now, but in time they will progress if you don't avoid further head injuries."

Fuck.

"That's your medical opinion?" I confirm.

He removes his glasses. "Yes. I've known you since you started with Coach Rusk. I wouldn't recommend this if I didn't think the risk was too high. I respect you as a player and a man. You're young. I'm sure someday you want a wife. Children." He shrugs. "That's my final recommendation."

"I appreciate it, Doc." I clear my throat. "Can I ask a favor? Let me tell coach. I'm not in Texas right now and I would prefer that conversation be face to face."

"Of course." He nods. "All of the reports are in your email and Heather will call you for a follow up."

"Thanks."

The screen blacks and I scrub my hand across my jaw. I was always waiting for *that* moment. The moment when all the stars aligned, and I could make everything right.

But you know what they say about the best laid plans.

CHAPTER 9

Tilly

Mornings are my favorite. When you just crack open your eyes. The world is still quiet. Your bed warm. That small moment in time when you can just lay there and pretend you don't have a million responsibilities. That moment when you forget all the bad things life has thrown at you. It takes your brain a minute or two to reset and then you're alerted. It ends all too soon.

Life isn't going to stop. The world keeps spinning whether you are ready or not.

The watch on my wrist vibrates, sending a jolt through my relaxed body. I glance down at the screen and see Blaine's name.

Pushing up on my elbows, I reach for my hearing aids that are charging on my night stand. Slipping them in, I snatch my phone up and answer as I pad to the bathroom.

"Hey." I smile.

"Morning, sweetheart." His voice flows through just as I flip on the light.

"When are you coming to town? Today?" I ask.

"Miss me?" He chuckles.

Do I? Or am I wanting a buffer?

I ignore the thought and answer accordingly. "Yes."

"I have meetings today with clients."

I sit down on the toilet seat.

"I'm driving my parents down Saturday evening for the dinner," he adds.

The dinner. Right.

We're having a family dinner this weekend. Blaine insisted our families meet. Which is fine. I've met his parents once. They seem nice. *Wealthy.* I was surprised they agreed to come to Timber Creek. Especially The Peak. It doesn't seem like their scene.

"Ok. Will y'all be staying the night?" I ask hopeful.

"No. I'll drive them back," he says before he's muttering to someone else in the background.

"Can't they just Uber and you stay?"

Because I need you to be the barrier.

Oh, because that worked so well last time, Tilly, I silently scold myself.

I close my eyes when he says, "Sorry, babe. I have a golf game scheduled with a new potential client Sunday morning. T off is at eight."

I huff out a sigh.

"This will all be easier when you move to the city," he says.

"I thought you were selling the condo?" I frown.

"I am, but I plan on buying a house near our main office."

"My job is here, Blaine."

"I know that. Not that you will even need to work. I want to take care of you, Tilly." He mutters something again before he continues. "I'm running late. I don't want to argue right now. We can discuss our living arrangement when I get there."

My eyes were focused on an empty bottle of conditioner I have yet to throw away. Something Blaine has reprimanded me for more than once when he's been in here.

"I don't want to argue either. Ok, call me tonight?"

"Of course."

He hangs up and I place my phone on the counter. There's so much we haven't discussed. But we have time. We have the rest of our lives to figure it out. Together.

Right?

When I step through the doors of the Timber Creek center this morning I feel a sense of peace. I always did here. It's where I thrived. Where I felt the most confident in myself. Jessie, the receptionist smiles and pushes her red rimmed glasses up on her nose.

"Morning, Tilly," she chirps.

"Morning." I slip past her desk, turning the corner to my office.

My first session wasn't until nine this morning. His name is Eli, and he was absolutely adorable. He's three years old and we're introducing the basics.

I toss my purse in its usual spot and fire up my computer. I had a semi busy day ahead, but I was grateful for it. I needed my mind to be occupied.

The hour passes quickly and before I know it my class with Eli is almost over. His blonde mop reminded me of a shaggy dog, and I couldn't help but give it a little shake when he gave me a hug goodbye.

"See you next week, Kristine." I sign in addition to speaking verbally, always wanting to encourage my students.

Eli is still young, but the more he experiences, the faster he will catch on.

Kristine gives a wave from the front door, hustling the toddler out into the cool weather. I shiver when the wind from the open door blows through the reception area. Turning, I run my hands up and down my arms, heading for my office when I halt my steps.

Through the window I have a clear view of our outdoor area. We would often hold classes outdoors when summer rolled around, but other times it was used for our volunteer outings. I took a few tentative steps closer to the window. Lifting my fingers, I reach up, separating the blinds so I can peer out at the group of young boys, and one professional football player.

I watch him crouch down in front of five awe struck eight-year-olds. His face is serious as he speaks to them, and it's clear each boy is hanging on to every word out of his mouth. A few of the boys give eager nods and he holds up his fist, letting each one get in a bump before they all take off running across the snow covered yard.

I lean slightly forward, watching as Greyson pushes to stand. He has a football tucked under his arm, and a genuine smile on his face. He always did when he was here. He had been volunteering in the off season since he was in college. I just usually made myself scarce that week. I had no idea he would be volunteering *now.*

His arm lifts, the brown ball clamped firmly in his palm. My traitorous eyes track every movement. The nod of his head, the way he slightly steps back onto one foot. The fluid motion of his arm raising to let the ball sail smoothly through the air. I'd watched this man play a hundred games. Maybe more, and it never failed to steal my breath when he had the ball in his hand. His *dream* in his hands.

I let out a quiet scoff. I should be preparing myself for my next class, not ogling the man I despise. One of the boys catches the ball and Greyson's hands clap together in encouragement. My heart warms to watch the boy beam from ear to ear as he returns the pass.

Just when I decide I've creeped long enough, Greyson angles his body back for another pass, only this time, those eyes are not trained ahead, they're trained on *me.* He makes the pass effortlessly without ever breaking eye contact. I hold his stare, challenging him like I always did. But in the end, it was me who broke the moment. I was hell bent on proving a point.

I was over him.

CHAPTER 10

Tilly
The past

It's been two months since we buried my mother. Sixty days since I've uttered a word. The first three weeks I even took out my hearing aids and just boasted about in pure silence. I just needed time to mourn in my own way. Time to work out in my head the reasons why cancer chose my mom. Everyone is dealing with the loss the best they can. Dad is vacant. Whitley is almost nonexistent; Camille is now in therapy and Adam is trying frantically to keep us all from dissolving away all while being a rookie cop.

I spend most of my time after school out by the lake. It's peaceful and I'm patiently waiting until winter rolls around and the beautiful water turns solid. That's when I'll skate. That's when I'll let the memories take hold and I'll let the wind blow through my hair as I picture her laugh.

I'm sitting under my favorite pine when I feel a presence at my back. I turn just in time to see Greyson, my brother's best friend, as he steps out from amongst the trees. I've known Greyson since I was a kid. He and my brother had become like brothers when his family moved here, which in turn somehow promoted him to act as mine as well.

"Mind if I join?" He asks.

My eyes follow the movement of his lips. It's become a habit. Even when I have my hearing aids in. I take in what's he's wearing. Some black joggers and a grey t-shirt that's soaked with sweat around the neck and down the front of his chest. It leaves nothing to my imagination.

I nod before tucking a piece of hair behind my ear. His steps are long as he crosses a few rocks to the clearing next to me. I watch him sit, still confused as to why Greyson Roy is out here. Sitting next to me in silence. He's home from college for the summer. As a college football player, it shocks me he still visits often. He's only a couple of hours away though, so I guess it makes sense. His entire family is here.

"It's nice out here," he says.

I glance over to see his profile. His jaw has a layer of rough stubble and he moves his arms, balancing them on his knees. The movement causes his biceps to bulge and for the first time in two months I actually feel something. A flutter. Deep in my stomach because I've always thought he was handsome, but up close. This close. He's gorgeous.

Masculine, gritty, and his hands....they're big and calloused. I momentarily forget what he said, but I blink, and bring my hands up to sign.

It's my favorite place.

He watches my hands, but I know he doesn't really know sign language. I've spoken to him a handful of times over the years, but I'm all of sudden very self-conscious. I know I sound different.

I'm staring at the lake when I feel his hand move towards me. He tugs at the bill of my Timber Creek PD cap. "You gonna let me hear your voice?"

His question causes me to blush and I flicker my eyes up to his face. His smile is genuine and I notice the beautiful gold flecks in his eyes.

Jesus those are pretty.

I shake my head no, and face the water again. I'm not ready.

"So, you got a claim on this place?" He motions around.

No. I shake my head again.

"Good." He pushes up to his feet, slipping his ear buds into his ears. "Same time tomorrow."

He takes off in a jog before I can respond. I already know that tomorrow, I glance down at my watch, at four-thirty PM, I'll be right here, waiting.

CHAPTER 11

Tilly

"You have got to be FREAKING kidding me," I shout out into the silent vehicle.

The entire day after I got caught being a peeping Tom was terrible. I had two students have complete meltdowns. The sole came off my favorite pair of boots and I spilled spaghetti sauce on my white sweatshirt.

I'm flustered over Blaine's lack of presence and irritated at Greyson's unwelcome arrival. My entire lunch hour was spent listening to four women who were supposedly "happily married" gossip about some vulgar and downright nasty things they would gladly do to the NFL superstar who just got to town.

Well, not my whole hour. I lasted about forty minutes before I couldn't take it anymore and I took out my hearing aids.

Now, I'm currently sitting on the side of the snow covered road. My car in the ditch and my breaks suddenly nonexistent. At least they were when I tried to miss the deer that darted out in front of me. They were fine at lunch, I'm not sure what happened between then and the four hours it was sitting in the parking lot.

When I finally catch my breath, and move my shaking hands, I glance out the window to see my entire hood covered in snow.

Awesome.

Grabbing my phone from my purse, I wretch open my door and climb out. My car is angled downhill, making the door swing back and almost smash me against the side before I dart out my arm to stop it.

I would only be able to accurately describe it as the legendary Edward Cullen move.

I gasp, squeezing my body from beneath it, but lose my footing and I end up with my ass planted into a large pile of snow. Now I'm soaking. *Perfect.*

Gritting my teeth, I stand before I'm tromping to the front of my car to attempt to lift the hood. For what I don't know. I have zero knowledge of motors.

The hood is bent as heavy smoke bellows out from underneath into the night sky, so I do the only thing I can do. Make a call.

I make the obvious one first. My dad.

It goes straight to voicemail. Three times. I move on to the next man I've always been able to count on. My brother.

He picks up on the second ring.

"Tills. What's up?"

I can hear muffled music in the background along with laughter.

"Hey, I'm sorry to bother you, but I'm in a bind."

"Are you hurt?" I can hear the panic pick up in his voice almost instantly.

"No, no. I'm fine. Maybe some whiplash. I tried to dodge a deer and my breaks went out. I'm stuck on the road. My hood looks like shit."

The wind all of a sudden picks up, so I make my way back around to my side of the car.

"Where are you?" He asks.

"I'm not far from town. Just past Tarver Road," I say as I shiver.

"Ok. I'll be there in ten."

He hangs up and I make the last step to my car and reach for the handle. I yank, but the door doesn't budge. I yank again and again, then I peer through the glass.

I could scream. I've locked my keys in my car.

I groan out loud and turn to rest my back against the door. Why is the universe torturing me?! *Probably because you let the man who broke your heart stick his tongue down your throat while your date was asleep in your bed.*

Touché. Universe. Touché.

I wrap my arms around my shoulders, trying to keep them warm by rubbing my palms along my hoodie. The temperature is dropping by the second and my breath is coming out in solid puffs of white smoke.

Beep.

No.

Beep.

Damn it.

With one last beep to signal the battery was out of juice, my hearing aids died. My frozen fingers pluck them from my ears, and I shove them in my front pocket. I let out a defeated sigh just as headlights appear up the road. Relief floods my system, but the feeling was only temporary. It was replaced with burning irritation when I saw who sat behind the wheel.

47

CHAPTER 12

Greyson

"What can I get you, Grey?"

The young blonde blinks innocently at me as she holds her notepad. I wasn't a dick, but only my friends call my me Grey. So, I give my best *I'm not interested* look and say. "Water and the grilled chicken plate. Grilled vegetables on the side."

She jots it down before turning to Adam.

"Officer Roy?" She smiles.

"Coke and the bacon burger. Extra cheese." He folds his menu then grabs mine. "Thanks Ashley."

She walks away and Adam smirks. "I see the ladies are still fond of you."

I bark out an amused laugh. "Sure."

"Still the love 'em and leave 'em motto?" He chuckles.

"I've never loved any of them," I quip.

Just your sister.

I pluck a pink sugar packet from the small holder in the middle of the table to keep my hands busy.

"Not even Anna Leslie?" He grins.

"Oh fuck, not you too," I scoff.

He laughs harder. "I'm joking. I know it's a crock."

I shake my head and fold the square in half. It's on the tip of my tongue to ask about his future brother-in-law. Thank God, he beats me to it.

"So, you heard the news?" He asks as Ashley places our drinks on the table.

"News?" I quirk a row.

"Tilly." He says with a pointed look. "Apparently she's marrying some city douche."

If Adam don't like him I sure as fuck won't.

"Yeah, that news. I'm aware." I take a gulp of my water to wash down the foul taste in my mouth. "Clearly you don't approve."

"Not really, but you know how she is." He shakes his head. "The more you push her the more she resists."

"Tell me about it," I mutter.

A serious expression crosses his face. "I know I've said it before, but you have no idea how much I appreciate you stepping in when I couldn't."

Not again. Not the thank you for being her other brother speech.

"I've never been able to get a handle on her. Dad either. You were the only one she seemed to listen to." He chuckles again.

"It's a gift." I shrug, trying to lighten the mood.

His phone pings with a text and he groans.

"Whitely is blowing me up. Tilly's avoiding her calls. I'm assuming to avoid the major ass chewing she's got coming, so now I'm in the hot seat."

He angles his phone to me.

Whit: WHY IN GODS NAME WOULD YOU ALLOW SOME PRISSY CITY PRICK TO PUT A RING ON HER FINGER. INTERVENTION IMMEDIATELY. IVE STALKED HIM. HE WEARS V NECK SWEATERS FOR FUCKS SAKE.

"She's a force to be reckoned with," I mumble.

"I feel bad for her future husband. Poor sap doesn't have a clue."

He isn't wrong. Whitley Harper is the one Harper sister who could probably take me.

He ignores the text, and we spend the next half hour eating and catching up while I let my nerves settle at the fact everyone seems to already hate this guy as much as I do.

"If you aren't busy tomorrow night, we're having a "family" dinner. I consider you family. You should come. We get to meet city boy's parents." Adam grins.

Dinner with my girl and the man she's promising to love for the rest of her years?

Sounds like a fucking picnic.

"I'm there. Send the details." I wipe my mouth with my napkin. "When does your shift end?" I ask.

"Midnight. It's been a pretty slow night." He drops his fork onto his plate after his last bite.

I fish out my wallet when his phone rings.

"Tills, what's up?" He answers.

I still, flicking my eyes up to his.

His brows pull together and he asks. "Are you hurt?"

My heart rate picks up.

After a few minutes he ends the call with "I'll be there in ten."

He pushes to stand.

"What's going on?" I ask.

"It's Tilly. She's stuck on the side of the road. She almost hit a deer. Car's in the ditch." He scrubs a hand down his face.

I pull out some cash and drop it on the table. "Need any help?"

"No man, I got it." He waves me off.

He wasn't three steps from the table when his walkie talkie crackled.

Unit, please respond to 700 Moss Ct. disturbance reported.

"Shit," he hisses as he silences it.

He turns to face me, and I already know. I've been doing it for years.

"I'll take care of her." I nod.

He slaps a hand on my shoulder and nods back. "Thanks, Grey. I owe you."

Chapter 13

Tilly

I narrow my eyes into slits as Greyson rushes towards me. His mouth is moving, I can tell from the glow of his headlights, but he's too far away and it's too dark for me to read his lips.

I haven't answered him, and without hesitation, he comes to a stop in front of me, reaching out, tucking a piece of hair behind my ear. His finger gently traces the shell, the gesture like it's second nature.

My ass may be frozen numb at this point, but heat radiates through my cold limbs at the one simple touch.

His hands lift as he signs. *You ok?*

I nod. Signing back, *yeah*. Then I tap my front pocket. *Hearing aids died.*

I shiver again and he immediately yanks his hoodie over his head, giving me a glimpse of a perfect V that leads to one of the only parts of him I haven't seen.

His hands are full, so I move my eyes to his lips.

"Lift," he commands.

My luck was pretty shitty tonight, and my teeth were chattering so hard I didn't even attempt to argue. I lift my arms, and he steps closer, sliding the hoodie over my small frame. It engulfs me, wrapping me up in the same smell that was always just so.... Greyson. His own special brand.

"You're freezing. Why are you standing out here?" He asks as his palms slide behind my neck, flipping my hair out from the hood.

I give him a look. *I just thought I'd enjoy a nice chill evening.*

He lifts a brow.

Fine. I locked my keys in the car. I admit, signing quickly.

His lip tilts slightly, as if he's reliving a memory. My stomach twists because I'm all too familiar with the same one. This wasn't the first time he's rescued me.

Instead of feeling nostalgic, I nudge past him and storm towards his truck.

I wasn't thrilled he was here, but I was so cold I probably would have jumped in with Ted Bundy himself. *I felt like I was close to death anyway.*

His large strides catch up with me, and he's latching onto the handle before I can get to it. He opens the door of his truck so I can hoist myself up. When I hit the seat, I notice he has on nothing but a thin long sleeve shirt.

I frown, and shift to remove the extra hoodie, but he stills my hands.

"No." He shakes his head.

I glare at him, but he just reaches over, buckling my seatbelt before he slams the door. He jogs around the hood before climbing in next to me.

Adam said you missed a deer? He signs.

Yes.

Short and to the point. That's the best way to keep it.

I'll have Tony pick it up in the morning. He signs before he shifts the car in drive.

Tony was the one and only mechanic in town. A sweet older man who worked magic on anything that ran on gasoline. Lawn mowers, cars, tractors, snow mobiles. The occasional *Barbie Jeep.* I grin thinking about the time I wrecked it. I hadn't had it a week. Camille was devastated and I ended up with a decent scar I was proud of.

I felt the graze of his knuckles on my arm, so I flicker my eyes over to him. "You look good in my clothes, Rosie."

I lift my hand, flipping him the bird before I cross my arms, and face the window. I don't care how cold I am, I'm not falling for the Greyson Roy charm.

I was beginning to thaw, but my wet jeans weren't helping. Greyson slows down and begins the entry to what I just now realized was the driveway to his parent's house.

I immediately brought my hands up. *What are you doing? Take me home.*

He ignores me, pulling up to the massive home on the edge of the mountain. I had been here a few times with Adam. It was beautiful and modern. The view was to die for.

"You're freezing. This is closer."

Before I knew it, we park and he's out of the seat and rounding the hood again.

I huff, rubbing my eyes with my palms.

Greyson opens the door and when I didn't step out, he moves at lightning speed, scooping me up before we're in route to the house.

I squirm, but it did nothing. He was like a cement wall of muscle. Sculpted and strong. I felt safe in his arms. I always had and that feeling confused me.

He sits me on my feet long enough to unlock the door, and I follow because at the moment all I have on me is wet clothes and a cell phone that was nearing its battery life as well.

The house is toasty, and a low fire is already burning in the fireplace.

He flips on a few lights, hits a few buttons on the coffee maker then he turns to face me.

He leans a hip against the counter and crosses his arms over his broad chest. "Strip."

CHAPTER 14

Greyson

The look on her face is priceless.

Excuse me? She signs.

I take a few steps and point behind her. "Bathroom is there. You need out of those wet clothes." I know she can read my lips in the light, so I don't sign.

I'm fine. She lies.

"Stop being stubborn. I'm not gonna watch you get undressed." I grin. "Towels in the cabinet. Take a hot shower and I'll get you dry clothes."

I turn and leave, before I do something I'll regret. *Like join her.*

I would never intentionally put her in that position. If I had known she had company the night I decided to get drunk and toss caution to the wind, I would have gone about it in a different manner. Regardless of how strong my feelings are for her, she's not the kind of person to cheat. Not after what happened to Whitley. She's very sensitive about it. I know she's probably already been wracking herself with guilt about the kiss.

Doesn't mean I enjoyed it any less.

I move through the house, turning on lights as I go. I jog upstairs to my old room and grab some sweats and a sweatshirt from my college days. I check the bottom drawer and grab the pair of socks I keep in the same spot. I guess I was just waiting for the day I could put them to good use.

I hear the bathroom door open just as I make it down to the kitchen. The coffee was done so I remove the pot and cross over to her. The door is barely cracked, and I can see her wild blonde hair when I approach. My gaze drops to her hands, which clings to a flimsy as fuck towel. *Is that a hand towel?*

I hold up the clothes inches away from the gap. I was coaxing along her next move.

She finally huffs in irritation, and pulls the door open enough to snatch the clothing from my hand, then slams the door in my face.

I chuckle and go back to making her coffee and putting a small pot on the stove to make her some soup.

My hands slightly tremble when I turn the dial on the stove. I tried my best to keep memories from that awful night at bay but seeing her freezing....and alone.

A twinge deep in my gut makes me wince. That night was all a disaster. One misunderstanding after another that led to me doing things I regret.

I brace my hands on the counter and take a deep breath. A throat clearing has me standing again, and I motion for her to sit at the table.

She pads through the kitchen with my sweats that are three sizes too big and lime green fuzzy socks. She casually sits down before lifting her hands.

I can't believe you still have these.

She lifts her leg, twirling her ankle around.

I shrug. "You gave them to me."

Her eyes meet mine and the only sound in the room is the boiling liquid of the chicken soup on the stove. A lone piece of blonde hair falls across her face and her lips purse, blowing it out of the way.

I clench the countertop, trying everything I can to avoid picturing those lips wrapped around my cock like I have on multiple occasions. I pour her soup in a bowl and pick up her mug of coffee. She watches me with a careful gaze as I place both items in front of her, then take a seat on the chair across from her. I rest my forearm on the table, watching as she wraps her hand around the warm mug. The diamond on her finger reflects from my kitchen light, reminding me how long I've been denying myself. Denying her. So, I meet her eyes and ask her a question.

"Have you called your fiancé?"

She freezes and I can see it all over her face. *She forgot about him.*

Just like any time we've been in the same room since she was seventeen. No one else existed.

CHAPTER 15

Tilly

What a dick.

Let me rescue you. Take care of you. But don't worry, I'll leave you here while I go back to my million-dollar house and super models in my bed every other night while you sit alone wondering why you ever thought you would be good enough.

I really did hate him.

He's in a meeting. I sign forcefully as I push to my feet.

I didn't have to sit here and eat his stupid soup and listen to him throw things in my face. *Things that make me uncomfortable.*

But you know why you're uncomfortable, Tilly.

"It's nine o'clock at night," he states.

I clench my hands before I sign. *It's a dinner.*

"I'm sure drinks and the exclusive strip club to follow? Isn't that how all those uptight socialites do?" He practically hisses.

You would know, wouldn't you? I shot back.

My feet carry me across the tile flooring and back into the bathroom. I dig around in my pile of clothes on the floor, searching for my phone. When I find it, I quickly type a message to my sister.

Me: can you please come pick me up at the Roy house. I will explain later.

Within seconds she was sending her reply.

Cami: on the way and no you don't have to explain.

I almost smiled; she was always so understanding. She's never been afraid to help me clean up my messes. I lock myself in the bathroom and wait. I wasn't going to deal with his hypocrisy. Like he wasn't draped across some random woman every other night of the week.

Fury got the best of me, so I sent Blaine a text.

Me: hey, just letting you know I got into a little accident. I'm ok. My car may not be, but just wanted to let you know I'm not home yet but will be soon.

I press send and blow out a breath. Maybe he'll come tonight. Stay with me. Help me get my car fixed. Do the things fiancé's do.

That was wishful thinking. My heart sank when I read his reply.

Blaine: Sorry babe. You needed an upgrade anyway. I prefer you drive a luxury vehicle.

What the ever loving fuck?

I rose to my feet. It's still new. Maybe that's his way of showing love. Gifts. He wants to get me a new vehicle. Something safe.

With defeated hands I gather up my clothes and finally unlock the door. Greyson still sits in the same place, thighs wide as he watches me with amusement. The soup sits on the tabletop along with the coffee. Guilt hits again. This time for a very different reason.

He's asked me if I was ok. Gave me clothes. Fed me, while my fiancé couldn't even send a concerned text message. I stop the emotions before they get out of hand. I was reading into it. Just like I did back then.

Camille sent a text to let me know she was here, so I face Greyson.

Did Adam ask you to come?

He didn't answer immediately, which was answer enough.

Again, he was dealing with me out of obligation and nothing more.

I nod. *That's what I thought.*

Then I slip on my boots and dart out the door.

CHAPTER 16

Tilly

"This is ridiculous." I throw the bland dress across the room and fall back onto my bed.

"Wow. I see the dramatics are in full effect today," Bekka quips from beside me.

I glare at her as she sips from a Starbucks cup. "Shouldn't you be…I don't know. Wedding planning. When are you and my brother getting hitched?" I ask.

"I told him, I don't care about all the fancy stuff. I just want this one venue. It's gorgeous. Very rustic. We were hoping for May, but they were booked so we're pushing it to fall."

All that just sounds like a headache. I groan and sit up from the bed.

"So…" she drawls out. "Adam mentioned you had car trouble last night."

"Yeah. Deer came out of nowhere," I mutter as I climb off the bed and go to my closet.

"Hmmm," she hums.

She's fishing, but I ignore her, rummaging through the hangers.

I received a text this morning from Greyson.

Grey: Your car is at Tony's. You might need an alternate ride the for the next week, so check your driveway. Keys should be in the floorboard.

I replied with a simple *thank you.* I didn't ask him to do all this.

Oh, that's right, my brother did.

And wouldn't you know. A freaking brand new Ford Bronco was in my driveway the next morning. Who just pulls a brand new vehicle out of their ass?

"Are you going to pretend Greyson didn't come get you?" She muses from behind me.

"Yes, but something tells me you aren't going to let me." I spin around and plant my hands on my hips.

She shrugs innocently. "He has good intentions, Tills."

I snort. "Right. Let me guess, he does 'what's best for me.'" I mock with air quotes.

I recall something very similar to the last words he said to me before stomping all over my heart.

Bekka's eyes are so kind I hate that I'm being harsh, but everyone gives him a pass. Everyone but me.

"It has to be beige." I announce, changing the subject.

She makes a face. "What has to be beige?"

"My outfit." I wave a hand at the dress that made me look like my great aunt Margaret.

"Why?" She laughs. "You are anything but *beige.*"

"I don't really know. Blaine just instructed me to dress "classy" and he would prefer beige. His mother would like it." As soon as I say the words, I want to reel them back in.

"You're joking right?" She gawks.

"Afraid not." I sigh.

My phone buzzes and another groan forces its way up my throat. I had been ignoring my older, very anti-relationship sister all week. She was still in California, working her way up the corporate ladder, but never let anything that happened here at home slip by her. Including this engagement.

"If you don't want her hopping a plane, I suggest you answer," Bekka deadpans.

I close my eyes before swiping the screen. I come face to face with Whitley Harper. She looks just like our mother when she was her age. Golden brown hair and hazel eyes.

"Hey Whit," I answer.

"Hey. Whit," she says with a blatant pause.

I almost flinch. "I've been meaning to call you."

She laughs as she lifts her glass of wine into view. "Oh, were you? I call bullshit."

I roll my eyes. "Ok fine. I was ignoring you."

"Yes. Because you know I've got ninety-nine problems and you marrying some random golf club collector shouldn't be one of them," she snaps.

How the hell did she know that?

"Don't give me that look." She points a manicured nail at the screen. "I've been reading up on ole Mr. McKnight."

I lift the phone away as she starts rattling off random facts that she learned from some unknown source. Bekka just shrugs as I bring the phone back to my face.

"I'm just saying. You've known the guy for five minutes. How do you know he's the one?"

I don't.

I frown at the first thought, but I push that aside. He is the one. I'm ready for someone to love me.

"Can't you just tell me congratulations like a normal person?" I scoff.

"I'm not trying to be the wicked bitch of the west here, but this is *marriage* Tilly. This is babies. Holidays. Compromises. Sickness. Money. No money. I just..."

She sighs and I can see the emotion build in her face.

Whitley doesn't do emotions often. "We had an extraordinary love story to watch growing up. The way mom and dad loved each other was...real. It was so..."

"Natural," I whisper.

"Yeah." She smiles. "I just want that for you. If you know without a doubt your love for each other is like *that.* I'll be your biggest supporter. But be sure, Tilly. This is your heart. Once it's broken......" she trials off

I know all about broken hearts, I want to say, but I don't.

"I know whit," I assure her.

Whitley's heart will never be the same. It's why she's so adamant that me and Camille protect ours. Why she will never give hers away again.

"I love you, Tills. I just want you to be happy," she says before she takes another drink.

"I love you too and it's not like we're getting married tomorrow, so, calm down." I laugh.

"Thank God," she mumbles.

"Bye." I wave before tossing the phone on the bed.

Bekka's face shows me exactly what I don't want to see. Doubt.

"So." I clap my hands. "Beige."

CHAPTER 17

Greyson

The Past

"You see the game last week?" I ask.

Tilly rolls her eyes and signs, I got better things to do, Pretty Boy.

She lifts her foot, shoving on her skate.

I bark out a laugh as my brows lift. Nerves swarm in my stomach. I'm not sure why. It's been doing that lately. Ever since I started this thing with Tilly Harper. Adam came to me desperate. He was worried about her mental health and his plate was stacked full. She always hated his overprotective nature, so he asked me to talk to her. Maybe she would listen to someone who wasn't her family. Someone who wasn't an authority figure.

That was four months ago. The summer slipped by quickly, and before I knew it was my final semester at Denver. I had been working my ass off to get ready for the draft, so my visits became less frequent, but it was the Holidays, and I was home for a small window of time. Instead of spending it with my family, I'm out here. With her.

She still hadn't let me hear her voice yet, but she was ok. She wasn't unstable or a danger to anyone. She was just grieving. She's going about it in her own way and one of those ways I'm learning is skating. I sit here for hours, watching her glide across Piper Lake like some kind of angel. Funny thing is she has no idea my mother use to be a competitive skater before she met my father.

I take a deep breath before I lift my hands and sign. Pretty boy?

Her eyes widen and a red tinge stains her cheeks as she stares at me. Her blue eyes glisten as she watches my hands fumble in the air.

Did I do it right? *I sign.*

For the last three weeks I had been taking an online ASL course at night. After class and practice, it was late as shit, but I was determined. If she wasn't comfortable enough to speak, I wanted to be able to communicate. To know her thoughts. Most of the time I talked, and she just laughed, smiled, signed something I couldn't understand, or sometimes said nothing all. But Tilly's heart always shined through in everything she did. Her determination. Which is why I loved to watch her skate. I could relate to the work ethic. She would spend an hour watching YouTube videos before she'd step on the ice and attempt the move. She wouldn't leave until it was mastered. I would shout the little things she needed to do. Squeeze your middle tighter. Pull that outer leg higher. I was forced to watch enough videos of my mother I could coach a whole damn team of figure skaters. Plus, I was competitive by nature, and I lived for training. Pushing.

My instincts told me I was getting too close, but when all I ever felt was pressure imploding on top of me, the only peace I have ever been able to achieve is when I'm here with her. On the lake.

When most eight year olds were hiking or riding bikes, my dad had me running drills. Memorizing plays and watching "film." I loved football. I dreamed of football. A career. To be able to follow in my father's footsteps. But that dream came at a price.

A bashful smile graces her face, and she lifts her small hands. Not bad. Someone's been practicing.

I chuckle and for some unknown reason I was fucking blushing. In front of a seventeen year old girl. My best friend's seventeen year old sister for that matter.

What the hell am I doing? Being a good friend. That's it. Getting her through her grief. For Adam.

She laughs, full on, with her head tilted back and I swear in that moment I had never heard anything more beautiful. So powerful. When her hair falls over her shoulder, I reach up, touching the shell of her ear.

You're not wearing them?

She shakes her head. They hurt my ears sometimes. I've had these a long time and I'm outgrowing them, but they're really expensive.

"Have you told your dad?" *I say and sign, just in case I screw it up.*

No. He's dealing with enough. I don't want him to worry. I'll be ok.

I watch her expression change as she looks out over the water.

I nudge her with my shoulder, and she glances over at me.

Tilana Rose Harper was more than she appeared. She was softer. There was vulnerability behind the girl who always rebelled against the given rules.

She pushed to her feet, grabbing my shoulder for balance before she places her blade on the ice.

Tell me Rosie, what's your dream? *I sign.*

I wasn't expecting the odd feeling to hit my chest when she looked at me. It was like I could see the word clearly. It danced in her pale blue eyes.

You.

And the fucked up thing about it was, for a second, I almost let myself feel the same.

CHAPTER 18

Tilly

"You look beautiful, sweetheart." Blaine grips my face in his smooth hands, planting a kiss on my lips.

"Thank you." I smile and run my hands over the hideous beige dress I paired with a blue jean jacket to make me feel halfway normal.

"I missed you. You ok from last night?" He asks.

"Oh, I'm fine. Car is at the mechanic. I rode with Adam and Bekka."

They had slipped in and went to the bar to meet Jace and Camille.

He nods then laces our hands together. "Can I talk to you for a sec?"

"Sure."

He leads me to the side of the building. "Mom insisted their driver bring them, so they should be here shortly."

"You could have come last night or this morning?" I ask.

"No, I was busy." He moves me in front of him.

"Doing what? I thought you just had a dinner meeting and nothing today?" I press.

His eyes rake down my body, and just when I think he's dying to get his hands on me, he reaches out, but it's not to touch me or pull me into him. It's to slip off my jacket.

"Let's get this thing off," he says as he shimmies it down my arms. "Better." He lays it over his elbow.

"Blaine, I asked you a question," I try again.

"I'm not sure why you're trying to pick a fight. I'm here, aren't I? Having dinner at this place with *your* family?" He waves a hand towards The Peak.

Am I starting a fight? On purpose? Maybe he's right. My brain has been scrambled since last night.

I close my eyes. "I'm sorry."

"It's fine. You had a rough evening. Now, I want to ask you something."

"Ok." I nod, already a little irritated that he just de-clothed me in public like I had on rags and refused to tell me what he was doing since last night.

"Can we try to speak verbally tonight?" His hand runs up my arm like I'm a child he's delivering bad news to.

"I'm sorry? What?" I tilt my head.

"I mean, my parents don't know sign language and I don't want to make them uncomfortable."

I'm almost stunned speechless.

"You don't know sign language. Does it make you uncomfortable?" I lift a brow.

"Of course not, babe." He leans into place a kiss on my forehead. "But my mother in particular can be a little, rash. She may see it as an imperfection, and I don't want her upsetting you."

I froze.

Imperfection.

Like I won't be good enough. Like me being deaf and wanting to sign in loud places is such a travesty.

"They do know I'm deaf, right?" I ask. "I mean, obviously I can hear with my hearing aids, but it's who I am, Blaine."

"Don't get upset." He pulls me in for a hug. "Yes, they know. I told them today."

"Today?" I croak.

"Yes. It wasn't a huge concern for me, but I did let them know in case they had questions."

I lean back, stepping away from his hold. "Why do I feel like you're ashamed?"

"I'm not." His brows crease. "And I don't want to discuss this any further. We are having a nice family dinner. You're dressed appropriately now. Let's go inside, keep your hands to yourself, and let's make a good impression."

He spins on his loafers and my jaw drops. Not because I have never seen this side of him before, but because Greyson stood just a few feet away.

And he was seething.

CHAPTER 19

Greyson

This motherfucker.

I was shaking so much with rage that Jace's face pales when I step into the restaurant.

"You alright man?" He lays a hand on my shoulder.

Jace was dating Tilly's sister Camille, and he worked with Easton and Adam at the station.

"I need a drink," I grit out.

I was three seconds away from wiping *Blaine's* face across the pavement. I would never do it in front of Tilly though. I would never want to scare her.

Imperfection.

The word alone has me clenching my fists. The fact he wouldn't even defend her to his own mother shows me exactly what kind of a man he his.

The bartender sets a glass down in front of me. I don't even ask what it is, I just gulp it down. The back of my hand swipes across my mouth and I feel a strong hand on my back.

"Long time no see, son." Richard chuckles.

"Cap." I smile and give him a hug, clapping him on the shoulder.

Richard Harper was the dad I never had. My father had the right intentions, he just lost sight. He tried to live through me, instead of allowing me to live my own life. Although we shared the love of the game, at one point, it became something I dreaded, instead of something I enjoyed. When that didn't fulfill him anymore, he knocked up his twenty year old mistress. *Asshole.*

"I heard about what happened with your dad." He shakes his head. "You need anything let me know."

I know he means the altercation. Who hasn't heard by now?

"I appreciate it." I nod.

He blends in with the crowd, and I turn, my eyes helplessly tracking Tilly as she glides across the room. Her dress shows off her curves, but it was nothing like what she would normally wear. Her hair was curled and pinned to one side at her temple. She was gorgeous, but something about the way she carried herself told me she hated it. She was a jeans and t-shirt kind of girl and I had yet to see another female take my breath away in just an oversized sweatshirt and a ball cap.

Blaine guides her to the table at the back that's reserved for all of us. I'm sure she thinks I'm just at the bar for a drink. She's about to be in for a pleasant surprise.

"He's a piece of work, isn't he?" I hear from beside me.

I glance down at Bekka who wraps an arm around my waist for a quick hug. "As far as Tilly is concerned, I'm supposed to hate you," she whispers. "But I know our girl is making a mistake."

Our girl.

I'm assuming Bekka was aware of our relationship. Or lack thereof.

I motion to the bartender for another round, because something is telling me I'm going to need it.

Bekka levels me with her eyes. "Fix it."

"Why do you think I'm here?" I grit out.

"I swear Greyson." She flares her nostrils. "I understand back then you did what you had to do, and she will never admit it…. but it hurt her. *You hurt her.*"

"You don't think I know that?" I shake my head.

"You've fucked around long enough." She glances over to the table. "She doesn't see it, but I see the red flags. The way he smooths things over. Gaslights her. It hasn't even been that long, and I can already see it."

"So why haven't you said anything?" I urge.

"Grey, you know her as well as I do. She has to learn on her own. She sees it as everyone coddling her. If I act like they do." She motions towards Richard and Adam. "I'll lose her."

"What about me? You think I won't?" I ask.

"It's been seven years. If you were going to lose her, you would have lost her by now," she says before she's heading toward the large table.

I haven't lost her? She's marrying another man.

Another drink is slid across the bar to me.

I toss back the shot then strut to the table. Maybe I can get through the appetizer without bashing in his face.

CHAPTER 20

Tilly

I was agitated. Hungry. And these damn underwear I had to put on with this ugly ass dress were pissing me off. Not to mention I just locked eyes with Greyson as he saunters to the table like he was actually invited.

"I hope you don't mind, I invited Greyson," Adam says as he steps over to hug me.

I'd rather get a lobotomy, but what the hell.

Camille and Jace walk over from the bar and my father greets me with a kiss on the cheek.

"Blaine." Dad shakes his hand.

"Mr. Harper. It's a pleasure." Blaine nods then moves to Adam. "Good to see you again, Adam."

Greyson leans across the table with a tight jaw. "I don't guess we've met."

Well, isn't he chipper.

"Holy shit. Greyson Roy." Blaine lights up and reaches for his hand. "Hell of a season, bro."

Greyson holds onto his hand a little too long, and apparently a little too tight because I hear Blaine grunt before he pulls back, shaking it off to the side.

"Thanks," Greyson deadpans.

"I had no idea you knew him." Blaine wraps an arm around my waist. "He's one of the best tight ends in the NFL."

"You watch football?" Jace asks with surprise.

Camille elbows him in the gut, but smiles. "That's awesome! You guys will have a lot in common."

"Yeah. I'm a fan." Blaine points to the seat across from him for Greyson to sit.

I resist an eye roll just as Regina McKnight comes creeping through the crowd with her husband Walter trailing behind. She's literally *creeping*. Like she's terrified to touch anyone or anything. Her mink stole is wrapped around her neck and she's wearing silk gloves. *And pearls.*

"Mom, dad," Blaine calls out, leaving my side to bring them to the table.

I take my seat, waving over Camille to sit next to me so I don't have to sit next to his mother.

I scoot my chair in and take a deep breath. When I glance at Greyson, he still has a murderous expression on his face and it's leading me to believe he heard our entire conversation outside.

Adam and Bekka take the seats next to Grey, and dad sits at one end of the table.

"Walter. Regina. it's so great to finally meet you." My dad stands just as they approach. "I'm Richard Harper. Tilly's father."

"Nice to meet you as well." Walter shakes his hand, and he lets Regina greet him with an awkward wave.

"Richard. You have a lovely daughter," she coos.

She comes up behind me, and not so subtly *yells* next to my ear. "Tilana, so good to see you!"

I wince away from her high pitch voice and pat the gloved hand that's resting on my shoulder with a smile.

The rest of the introductions are made and we're all finally seated, and drinks have been ordered. My nerves are all over the place. Number one, we're in public, number two, our families couldn't be more different and three, need I even say it. The brood that just *accidentally* slid his foot next to mine under the table then winked at me. *Actually winked.*

I'm going to need a lot of alcohol to make it through tonight.

The food finally arrived forty-five minutes later. It took Regina a solid ten to order because there were no vegan choices. *Never mind the animal that died she's got draped over her chair.*

"So. Tilana." Regina clears her throat, gaining everyone's attention. No one calls me Tilana. Not even my family. "Can you hear me ok?"

Blood rushes to my cheeks, and I nod, instinctively lifting my hands to sign because I want to crawl out of my own skin. But Blaine's hand lands over my mine, just as I begin to sign, and he presses them to the table. His eyes flicker to me in a scolding manner.

"Yes." I swallow, moving my hands out from his and pick up my glass of water.

"Blaine tells me you booked May third for the wedding." She smiles.

I practically choke on the water I just ingested. I cough, pressing a hand to my chest as Blaine rubs my back. "We actually." I cough again. "Haven't set a date."

"Oh?" She gives her husband a glance. "They called to confirm the deposit this morning."

I turn to Blaine who smiles nervously. "Baby, it's a beautiful place and that was the only date available. Plus, why wait?" He reaches to touch my cheek. "We're in love, right?"

That's in five weeks.

I feel dizzy. The room is spinning. I may actually pass out.

"Refills anyone!"

Thank God the waitress breaks the tension, so I face the table. "Blaine and I will discuss the date and I will let everyone know." I could feel him grip my thigh under the table, digging in his fingertips to show his disapproval.

My dad gives me a questioning look, but I smile to appease him. It's only when my eyes meet Camille's my heart sinks. She can see right through me and doubt has never been so present in my whole life.

CHAPTER 21

Greyson

I've never felt pure anger like this. When Blaine kept her from signing. Kept her from doing something that brings her comfort and security I almost dove across this fucking table. I order another drink, and Adam seems about as impressed as I am with this family.

I move my boot to the right, grazing Tilly's heeled foot to get her attention. *You ok?* I sign.

She nods, signing *yes* too quickly for my liking.

"What do you think Greyson?"

Blaine's voice draws my attention to him.

"What was that?" I ask.

"The bowl? I think y'all are in this next season."

"That's the plan." I shrug.

Isn't it always?

"You're a hoss. Four thousand and forty-eight rushing yards last season." He shakes his head and places his arm behind Tilly on her chair. "That game against the Dolphins was epic."

"Four thousand and fifty-eight." A voice interrupts.

I pause, flicking my gaze over to Tilly.

"What?" Blaine chuckles.

"He had four thousand and fifty-eight rushing yards," she corrects.

That's my girl.

"Same thing," he mutters. "That win was by a hair though." He whistles. "You almost didn't make that last touch down. Got a little too confident, yeah?" He barks out a laugh.

This fool looks like the only game he's ever played is croquet.

"I did my job." I gulp the last of whatever is in my glass and drop it back to the table.

"Still..." He runs his hand up over Tilly's shoulder and I can't help but let my eyes catch the movement.

He doesn't miss the fact I noticed and judging by the smirk on his face, he knows I don't fucking like it.

"He actually ran the route perfect. If Baxter would have blocked like he was supposed to, Krew wouldn't have rushed the pass. It was a sheer miracle Grey even caught it and then he ran a thirty-seven-yard touchdown," Tilly interjects.

The table goes silent and so does Blaine.

My eyes meet hers and she blushes before snatching up her drink. I watch her throat work as she takes in the liquid. I wonder what the skin there would taste like? I wonder what *she* would taste like?

My eyes never leave hers as Blaine mumbles something in her ear before he's on his feet, guiding his parents away from the table.

Call me cliché, but I'm now internally beating my chest like some possessive caveman. She once told me she doesn't watch football.

Looks like my Rosie is a dirty little liar.

Apparently spending the evening watching the woman I love get shit on by her future husband and in-laws wasn't enough. My phone pings with and message.

Krew: hey man, May tried to squash this one quick, but it's spreading like wildfire. Just a heads up.

I click on the link that leads to an article.

NFL player Greyson Roy's father pressing criminal charges.

Bastard.

Me: thanks. I appreciate it.

I scrub a hand down my face as I sit with Adam and Jace at the bar.

"More bullshit?" Adam asks.

"Yeah. It's never ending."

Dinner dispersed about an hour ago, and the men, minus Cap and the man who had Tilly holed up in the corner, arguing, were nursing a few beers.

Blaine is trying to be subtle, but I know her tells. She's pointed that angry face at me every time I've came to visit over the years. Granted I deserved it. *So does he.*

I finally see her give him a less than affectionate hug, and Bekka drags her to the dance floor. He heads out the front door and before I know it, I'm on my feet.

"Grey?" Adam calls.

I ignore him and stalk out onto the sidewalk. I glance left before I spot him to my right, looking down at his phone. I've got a few inches on him so I can see the busty brunette with barely any clothing on he's texting not two minutes after kissing his fiancé goodbye.

"Hey, Blaine," I call.

He locks his screen and turns. "What's up?"

"Can we talk?" I nod toward the side ally.

"Of course."

I have money, but I don't flaunt it. I don't dress like this shit head either. I watch his leather loafers collect snow as he tries to avoid the puddles.

As soon as we're in the clear, I take a step, pinning him hard against the brick.

"Let's get one thing straight, you sorry piece of shit," I grit out. "If I ever catch you talking to her that way again. Making her feel inferior for being different, I'll break every bone in your fucking body."

"Are you threatening me?" He tries to free himself.

My forearm crushes his windpipe, and I push harder. "No threat here. Facts."

His eyes bulge as I press harder, then release him. "Show her some respect and learn to read a damn room."

He gasps for air, and bends at the waist. I turn, storming back to the bar when I hear is voice. "How does it feel?"

I pause. "Come again?"

He stands, adjusting his collar. "How does it feel to know you'll never have her? Not like I will."

His arrogant grin spreads and I take another step back towards him.

"She may wear that ring on her finger." I brush my chest right up against his. "But make no mistake, *bro*." I toss back the sentiment he gave me earlier. I point my finger to the bar. "That woman. That beautiful, intelligent, strong willed woman has always been mine. I don't give a fuck if she has your last name, lives in your fancy house, or tolerates your bullshit." I step back, dropping my hand. "And as I said earlier in our conversation, that's not a threat, it's a fact."

The arrogance drifts from his face and I leave him standing in the cold alley, rolling over my words. Good. He better catch on quick.

CHAPTER 22

Tilly

The entire evening has been a disaster. I was fuming. If I wouldn't have been in such a public place I might have flipped the table.

May third.

He booked our wedding for May fucking third and didn't even bother to ask me or even tell me. He just assumed I'd play right along like the good little wife he thought I wanted to be.

We argued for thirty straight minutes. Blaine was a lawyer, so it was a pointless fight and instead of kneeing him in the balls for making me look like an idiot in front of everyone, I agreed to at least see the venue this week. He apologized profusely and thought I would love the surprise.

Since he's paying for it.

His exact words. I was also still pissed about the signing comment. He knows that loud places make it more difficult for me so that's one of the reasons I often sign. It's easier and you would think marrying a deaf person would make you want to learn ASL, but he hasn't even offered. Not once.

The more I thought about it the angrier I got, and I had a harsh reality set in. Was Cami right? Was I making a huge mistake?

∗ ∗ ∗

By the sixth shot, the events of this evening were long gone from my mind and my body was buzzing. Bekka and I had danced song after song and Camille finally tuckered out about an hour ago.

These underwear were still riding up in all the wrong places, so I leaned over to Bekka, yelling over the music. "I'll be right back."

I moved through the crowd, and down the hall to the bathrooms.

"Tills!" Someone shouted.

Lucy came towards me and from the looks of it, she was about as buzzed as I was.

"Hey girl." She flung herself at me, gripping me in a sloppy hug.

"How was dinner?" She asks.

"Terrible." I laugh. "Which is why I can't remember how many shots I've had."

"Same." She waves at someone over my shoulder. "Have fun. If you need a ride home tonight just holler."

"Will do. Bye Luce."

She leaves me to join whoever she came with. The hallway was swaying and I had to lean up against the wood planked wall to get my footing. I blink a few times as I push into the next door. These panties had to go. *Now.*

I yank up my dress, clawing at the God forsaken fabric that was digging into my lady parts. I manage to grip the side and I begin to shimmy them over my thighs. My balance was off due to the tequila, so I settle one hand on the counter as I work one side of the waist down to my mid thigh. I groan, swaying as I switch hands and maneuver the other side down.

I was clearly struggling, but my hands halt all movement when I hear a voice from behind me. "Need a hand?"

I look up, glaring at Greyson in the reflection of the mirror.

"Why are you even in here?" I scoff. I make a show of looking around him. "Keeping up your reputation? How would Ana feel about you getting your rocks off in the girl's bathroom at a bar?"

I internally wince, but keep my facial expressions void of *give a shit.* I haven't mentioned Ana since he's been here. I didn't want him to think I kept tabs. That I even cared. But I was angry. And he was always the easiest person to release it on.

"First of all, this is the men's room." He cocks a dark eye brow.
Well shit.

"Second, Ana Leslie is nothing to me. Never has been, never will be. That's the media doing their bullshit." He takes a step towards me and I back up, planting my ass against the counter. My panties were still half way down my legs and he knew it.

"And third." He continues. "As I said, Ana would feel nothing about what I choose to do with my cock, so seeing as you're the only woman in this bathroom with me, are you offering?"

My jaw gapes open and I let out a scoff. "I would never," I sneer.

That sneaky grin spreads across his face. "Never say never, Rosie."

My hands grip the counter as he takes a step closer. I can feel the heat from his body as he slowly kneels down in front of me.

"Lift your dress," he commands.

My eyes widen. "No."

He shot me a pointed look. "I'm not going to touch you. I'm helping you so you don't break your neck in these heels."

Keeping my gaze on him, I lift my dress slightly. Just enough to reach where my underwear was sitting right above my knees. It was a bold move, but I was testing him. Or maybe I just felt like playing with fire. I couldn't really tell at the moment. My heart was beating entirely too loud for me to comprehend my actions.

His fingertips grip the fabric that stretches across my spread legs and I feel the material slipping down my skin. The lace hit my ankle and his eyes darken a fraction when he says.

"Step out."

I follow his command, stepping one heel out before the other.

I was practically panting. Sweating at the tension that swirled around us like a hurricane itching to make landfall. He picks up the scrap of material, standing to his full height first, before he shoves it in the pocket of his jeans.

"I told you I wouldn't touch you." His voice was thick. Heavy.

And he was right. He never touched *me*.

He glances down at my hand. My *left* hand. "Not with that ring on your finger." He steps to me.

Any closer and his lips would meet mine.

I felt his next words all the way down to my toes. "But when it's gone. I make no fucking promises."

CHAPTER 23

Greyson

Tilly was drunk and even though all she slung at me were insults, it's the first time since I've gotten to town she spoke directly to me. *Gave me her voice.*

I took my seat back at the bar, next to Adam. It didn't occur to me until now that I'm sitting next to my best friend, with his sister's panties in my front pocket.

That may have been a bad idea. Now my dick's hard.

"Adam, I'm tired." Bekka lays her head on his shoulder, and he kisses her temple.

"Okay, let's wait for Tills."

"Grey, would you mind dropping her home since it's on your way?" Bekka grins and shoots me a wink.

"I don't mind at all." I hold my hand out to Adam who shakes it as he nuzzles Bekka under his arm.

"You sure?" He questions.

"Absolutely." I nod.

"Alright, man I'll call you tomorrow." He waves as they weave through the crowd.

I shift my gaze back to the bathroom and spot her walking towards the bar. Her eyes scan until they land on me. She pulls her shoulders back and marches straight towards me.

I'm assuming I was left under your supervision again? She signs.

Her eyes were glassy, and she places a hand on the bar stool next to her to hold herself steady.

"Time to go." I slide a hundred dollar bill to the bartender and point for her to lead the way.

It's silent as we walk to my truck, and by the time we make the drive to the small cabin she's called home for the last four years, she's almost asleep. Her head is resting against the window as I park my truck and hop out.

When I gently open the door, she stirs and when her eyes land on me, it's like she's reliving all that anger all over again.

Her brows pull together and she swats away my offered hand. "I don't need your help. I haven't in a very long time."

I guess it's going to be that kind of night.

She climbs down from my truck, almost twisting her ankle as she attempts to navigate through the melting snow along the sidewalk.

Her hands fumble with her keys before she finally unlocks the door. When she pushes through, she stumbles again, hitting the hardwood floor on her knees.

Her security alarm is blaring, so I quickly cross the room, punching in the code I'm not supposed to know before the alarm can sound.

I'm back at her side in an instant, reaching down to help her when she pushes away from me. "I'm fine."

"Rosie, let me hel..."

"No," she snaps. Her hands travel down, removing her heels before they're sailing across the living room, knocking over a lamp in the process. "Leave me alone, Greyson."

"I'm just making sure you get in safely."

"Ha!" She staggers up to her feet. "Just being the obedient best friend, huh?"

Here we go.

"Poor Tilly can't handle herself. Poor Tilly needs someone to talk to. Poor Tilly is so rebellious. Poor Tilly is going to end up marrying into a miserable family..." she shakes her head and brushes past me. "I don't need anyone!" She shouts. "I don't need *you*. I don't need you pretending to give a shit about me. You left!" Her voice is rising with each word that slips past her lips.

"Till..." I start.

"You. Left. Me." Her voice cracks.

I can see the tears as I move towards her.

"Don't come any closer." Her hands fly up.

Fuck. I did this to her.

"You're drunk. We aren't doing this now." I take a step to her.

Mascara filled tears roll down her face, then her hand flies to her mouth. Her eyes widen just as she darts to the bathroom off the living room.

My eyes close when I hear the toilet lid flip up and she starts to vomit.

With guilt and remorse riddling my bones, I step into the half bath, grabbing a washcloth in the cabinet before I'm running it under the water. She heaves again and I pull her hair away from her face, dropping the washcloth on the back of her neck.

My palm rubs soft circles on her back, and all I want to do is take care of her. Wrap her up in my arms and apologize over and over for being gone. Apologize for making her think I didn't care. *That I didn't love her.*

When her head rests against her forearm, she groans.

"You done?" I ask.

Her eyes are closed, but she shakes her head yes. I could tell the fight had left her, so I pick her up and carry her upstairs. I remove her hearing aids, placing them on her charger, then put her to bed.

I wasn't leaving. I sat next to her, watching every breath she took. Wondering how the hell I can make things right. Make her see that it's always been her.

CHAPTER 24

Tilly

My eyes blink open, followed by a pounding sensation behind my eye sockets.

Geez.

I roll over, pressing my face into my pillow as I try to remember exactly how many shots I took last night.

The dinner.

Blaine.

My panties.

I shot up the second the smell of bacon hit my nostrils.

Who the hell was cooking bacon?

Last night's turn of events starts to play across my brain like a bad picture show. *I cried.* And puked. In front of Greyson.

Glancing down at the dress I still slept in, I tug it off, grabbing the hoodie laying at the foot of my bed. I slide myself into some leggings and dress my feet in my favorite fuzzy socks. I brush my teeth, splash some water on my face and tie my hair up.

With light steps I ease down the staircase, checking on Nelson as I pass his cage at the foot of the stairs.

Greyson's back is to me. The short sleeve tee he wore clinging to every muscle that rippled along his back. His jeans hung low on his hips and his hair was messy. He flipped a few pieces of bacon as he sipped a cup of coffee. Like this was his normal morning routine. *All domestic and shit.*

All my daydreams of what a life with Greyson would look like actually looked a lot like this. Sadly, I'll never know, and I've come to terms with it. Three days ago, I would have said I knew what my life was going to look like for the most part. But it's amazing how quickly things can change. How words and situations can shine light on things we couldn't see. *Or we choose not to see.*

I move the bar stool and the sound of the legs scraping against the hardwood steals his attention.

"Hey," he breathes out as he faces me.

Hey. I sat down, tugging the sleeves of the hoodie.

His eyes move from my face to the hoodie, then back again. I knew it was his. The one he gave me just two nights ago. It made me feel safe. Just the scent alone made it seem like I was wrapped in his arms, and though I had only been wrapped in them a time or two, I had never felt more seen or validated in my life. I guess I just needed that right now.

He sat down his cup, before grabbing a bottle of medicine from the cabinet, popping out two pills. He places the pills and a bottle of water in front of me.

"You already gave me your voice last night, Rosie. Don't get shy on me now."

I roll my eyes, then twist the top, and swallow the pills.

"You stayed?" The question came out before I could stop it.

He pauses, then fishes out the bacon with a spatula, placing it next to a pile of eggs he had already made. "You needed me." He shrugs.

I roll my lips together. "I was fine."

"Tell that to your lamp." He chuckles.

I turn on my stool to survey the damage.

"I already cleaned it up." A plate drops down in front of me. "Eat."

"Still bossy, pretty boy?" I quip.

I bite my tongue, inflicting punishment on myself for letting the nickname slip. It was just the smell of this food, and I was famished. That was all. My body wasn't fully functioning yet. My brain not fully awake.

He didn't comment on it, which I was thankful for, but he veers the conversation to something even less appealing.

"So, you really going to marry him?" He asks, tossing a spatula in the sink.

"Are you going to marry Ana Leslie?" I lift a brow before stuffing a piece of bacon in my mouth.

"Hell no," he scoffs.

"Hmmp." I chew. "Oh right, I forgot, you don't really do the whole serious thing. I mean, you seem to change women about as often as you change your underwear."

He leans down, pressing his forearms to my counter. The look in his eye unsettles me. It makes goose bumps coat my flesh when he smirks.

"Rosie, if I didn't know any better, I'd say you were keeping tabs on me."

"Oh please. You're splattered across every news outlet in Colorado, not to mention on social media. It's kind of hard to miss," I point out.

"I thought you didn't watch football either?" That smirk grows wider as I curse myself for opening my big mouth last night.

But I couldn't help it. It was like word vomit. I had this intense urge to defend him, which was absurd. I don't even like him. *Lie.*

"It was one game," I mumble.

He leans in closer. "Since you never answered my question, I'll ask an easier one."

God, he smelled good. It was throwing off my senses.

His eyes hold mine. "Do you love him?"

I slide off the stool. "I'm not having this conversation with you."

He lifts a shoulder. "Why not?"

"Because it's none of your business!" I snap. "You can't just blow into town on a whim and show up demanding answers from me." I snatch up the plate, dumping the remaining crumbs in the trash.

"*You* are my business." He pushes up from the counter. "You've been my business since the first day on that lake."

My gaze whips to his. "Don't. Don't you dare."

My hands grab angrily at the skillet, tossing it in the sink. "You made it crystal clear. You made that choice, so deal with the consequences."

"I did what was right," he grits out.

I glare at him over my shoulder. It infuriated me how beautiful he was while still continuing to be so damn difficult.

"Thank you for breakfast, but I have it from here, you can leave." I face the sink, praying he would just walk out.

I feel him watch me dunk a plate under the water. I was a stress cleaner. A little trait I inherited from my mother.

"I will never apologize," he states.

"Of course you won't." I laugh, shaking my head.

I felt the warmth from his chest at my back, the tickle of his breath fanning down the back of my neck. "If you'd quit running your mouth for two seconds and listen, what I was going to say was." He pauses, grazing his nose along the sensitive spot behind my ear. "I will never apologize for doing what's best for you." We both still and I close my eyes. "I know you don't see it Rosie, and I may have done a shit job of showing you, but *everything* I have ever done was always with you at the front of my mind."

His words settle on my wounded heart like a blanket, and I felt the tears well. I hated how good his words made me feel. I didn't want to *feel* them at all.

The heat behind me disappears and without another word, he walks out the door, leaving me even more confused than I was last night.

CHAPTER 25

Tilly

Waverly's blonde curls bounce as she jumps up into my lap. We finished her last class today and I was filled with both pride and sadness that she had completed the course.

You proud? She signs, her little cheeks round and full as she grins up at me.

So proud. I sign back before wrapping her up in a big hug.

Like me, Waverley was born deaf, but the little girl in my lap has mastered her classes and at four years old, she's a pro. She caught on quicker than any child I've taught, and it fills my heart that this is my job. That I have this place.

I met my boss, Dixie, when I was just a little younger than Waverley. She not only taught me how to communicate with my hands, but how to embrace who I was. When I was old enough, I started to volunteer, and when I was graduating high school, I knew exactly what I was called to do. Teach.

To help people just like me find their voice. Whether that be verbally or by the use of ASL.

Waverley's mom steps into my office and the excited little girl was already skipping across the carpet to meet her embrace.

"You've been a God send. You know that right?" She says as she gives me a look that holds nothing but gratitude.

"I'm just a girl who's excellent at talking with her hands. Nothing more." I laugh, signing at the same time so Waverley can be in on the conversation.

"I mean it. Thank you, Tilly," she says as moisture fills her eyes.

"None of that!" I wave a hand and push to my feet. "I have a no tears rule."

She laughs and sets Waverley down long enough to hug my neck. "Don't be a stranger. We would still love to see you."

"Absolutely! My door is always open." I glance down and tug on one of Waverley's blonde curls.

Stay cool, Wave. I sign.

Stay cool, Ms. Harper. Her little fingers move quick and then they're off and out the door.

My phone pings with a message from Blaine. I was supposed to be meeting him in the city at three to see the venue like I agreed. A nagging part of me told me not to go, but I had gave him my word and I hated to fall back on it. I wanted to give him the benefit of the doubt. Maybe he really was trying to be genuine and surprise me with a beautiful venue. It had been a few days since dinner and I was convincing myself it was a fluke. Maybe he had an off night. We all have our moments, but deep down I knew what that nagging feeling was. I knew what my heart was trying to tell me, but all that ever got me into was trouble. All it ever got me was insecurities. I wasn't going to just let go of every single feeling of self-doubt I had accumulated over the years. So, I cleared my head with an iced latte, then hit the road.

When we enter the gates to Mountain Escape, we're met with soaring pine trees and gorgeous mountain views. Snow still blankets the ground, but in just a few weeks, when May rolls around it will be green, and spring will be in the air. Blaine parks us close to the front and we walk hand in hand to meet a tall slender woman in a white pant suit. Suzette leads us around, showing us every aspect of the "included package" and while all of it was beyond what I ever thought my wedding would be like, I just....I wasn't ready to move this fast.

It's not the place.

Or the time frame.

You know what it is, Tilly.

I shut off my inner thoughts and manage to smile and keep my mouth closed until we make it back to the condo.

"Blaine...it's a wonderful place, but I just." I suck in a breath as we enter his kitchen. "I don't see why we have to rush."

"What do you mean?" He clanks a glass on the counter before he reaches for a bottle of whiskey. "You accepted my proposal."

"I did." I grip the back of his dinning chair that probably cost more than my cabin. "But I thought this was something we would decide together. Not you and your mother going behind my back."

"I would think you would be a little more grateful. Do you know how much that deposit was?" He scoffs.

"Grateful?" I roll my lips. "I don't want to get married in May. It's too soon."

"Tilly. I'm the one paying for this. You accepted the ring, so your duty as a wife starts now." He jabs a finger into the quartz countertop. "I'm funding it, so I call the shots."

Duty?

I release the chair. "This is supposed to be a decision we make together. And while we're on the topic, I didn't appreciate the spectacle at dinner, announcing it to everyone while I was out of the loop."

He knocks back a drink. "I think you're being dramatic."

What the hell has gotten into him?

"Dramatic? Well, here's dramatic for you. I *will* sign when I feel like it. You knew when you met me that it was a part of my life. A part of who I am."

"My world is different and I'm just preparing you for it. It's ruthless and I won't have a partner who's seen as weak."

That fucking does it.

"Weak?" I let out a tortured laugh. "Fuck you." I turn, walking to the door.

There's that gut feeling.

"What do you think you're doing?" He asks calmly.

I stop short of the foyer. "I think we need to slow down."

"Tilly." His nostrils flare as he practically growls my name.

An unfamiliar gleam twinkles in his eye that makes a chill run down my spine.

All my alarms bells go off.

"I'm going home." I turn to leave when I feel his grip on my upper arm.

"You don't walk away from me." His hand tightens, his fingertips digging into my skin so hard I know it will bruise.

"You're hurting me, Blaine," I hiss.

With a hard shove, he spins me, slamming me against the kitchen wall. Pain sears through the back of my skull, leaving a dull ache.

I meet his wild eyes. He looks deranged. Like a completely different person before it suddenly disappears. He immediately tugs me to his chest. "I'm sorry." He apologizes quickly. "That was uncalled for."

Uncalled for?

I couldn't breathe. I never had someone physically hurt me. Put their hands on me.

I was frozen in place and confused on his shift in behavior. He's never been aggressive towards me in any way.

His hand smooths down my back and he presses a quick kiss to my hair. "Now." He pulls back, looking down at me with concern. "It's been a long day. How about you go home, soak in a hot bath and tomorrow we can take a look at the calendar for a new possible date?"

The tension was gone from his body, so I slightly relaxed, giving a timid smile because I knew that's what he wanted to see. "Ok."

I step away uneasy, still trying to figure out what just transpired in the matter of a few minutes.

"Drive safe." His phone rings, and he pulls it up to his ear to answer.

With a wave of his hand, he starts his conversation, sending me on my way like he didn't just slam me into a solid wall.

With shaky legs, I step out into the hall and that inner voice that has been screaming since I let him slide this ring on my finger starts up again, but this time, I was actually quiet enough to listen to her.

CHAPTER 26

Greyson

My fingers pinch the bridge of my nose. It's been three days since I've seen Tilly. All I've done is workout, look over emails from my doctor, and dodge calls from Mavery. I know she's doing her job, but I don't want to take part in planning some bullshit story line about my nonexistent love life.

"Look! They're perfec!" June beams.

I glance down at the pink nail polish that's smeared all over my toes.

"You like them?" I ask.

She nods with a huge smile. "Pink is my favorite."

"Oh, aren't those cute!" Elle chirps and before I can contest, she snaps a picture.

"Eloise," I grit out.

"What?" She blinks innocently.

Elle can be downright devious.

I narrow my eyes. "I expect that to be deleted."

"Of course." She grins.

Easton chuckles as he passes by her. "Baby, stop messing with him."

"I'm just taking a sweet picture between a girl and her uncle." She waves a hand dismissively.

"You're racking up your blackmail file," he deadpans.

"What's blackmail?" June asks.

"Nothing," me and Easton say at the same time.

"I'm pretty sure she has a file on everyone," he mutters.

"He doesn't and calls himself a cop?" She scoffs. "Amateur."

I laugh as June bounces over to Elle in the kitchen.

"So, how long you staying?" Easton asks as he settles in the recliner.

"As long as it takes." I place my arm on the back of the couch.

As long as it takes for me to make sure she doesn't marry this ass hat.

"We both know she won't make it easy," he points out.

"She's worth it." I shrug.

"East! I'm about to head to Camille's." Elle shouts as she comes down the hall. "We got a code red text."

"Ah. Code language," Easton muses.

"I'm sure Jace was being an ass, or it involves Tilly." She flings her purse on her shoulder.

I push to stand. "What's wrong?"

She places a hand on my chest, pushing me back down. "Calm down. It's just girl talk. If your services are required, I'll let you know." She saunters over, dropping a kiss on my brother's lips.

"Be careful." He watches her leave and I realize If I've been looking at Tilly the way he looks at her, I don't know how the hell Adam has missed it all these years.

When the door closes, he faces me again. "How's the media?"

I hike my ankle up over my knee. "Typical."

"You talked to dad?" He asks.

"Since I almost killed him? No." I focus on a spot across the room.

"You know I appreciate you defending me, Grey, but don't ruin your career over his mistakes." His voice was even, but I could hear the emotion.

"My career is coming to an end anyway." I felt the squeeze in my chest at the words.

I hadn't told anyone about the doctor. Coach wasn't even fully aware yet. I wasn't sure what to do with the information. I could chance it. Try one last year for the bowl.

"You're still young. You got what? At least another five years in you?" He says.

"CTE." I let out a breath. "I'm well on my way if I don't step back now."

The room is silent. The only sound I could hear was the faint music flowing from June's TV upstairs.

"It's serious?" He clears his throat.

"Yeah. Could be. Doc is advising I retire early to avoid any more damage that could lead me down that road." I lift a shoulder. "I haven't even had time..."

"To live," he interrupts.

"I've loved football. Breathed, ate, slept, and played the game. I want more East. While I still can," I admit.

He nods. "Then I suggest you go get your girl."

I sit on the front porch of Tilly's cabin. My leg bouncing as anxiety sifts through every muscle in my body. I could have easily gone inside the locked door, but I wasn't really ready to reveal that secret yet. I've kept a lot of secrets from her over the years, but all were for her own good. I have always thought *one day*. One day when she had graduated college and began her dream job teaching at the Timber Creek Center. When my career was in full swing. When I could tell Adam the truth. But time just slipped away.

Tires crunch in the snow and headlights flash across my face. She pulls up slowly, then climbs out of the car. Her long legs move towards me, and I still have never felt a pull so strong to anyone else to this day.

"What are you doing here?" She frowns.

"Can we talk?" I push to my feet.

Her gaze follows me, then she hesitates, her eyes meeting mine before she nods.

When we step inside, she shrugs off her coat, sitting her purse on the table that's piled with mail.

I run my palms down my jeans when she turns to face me. Her arms cross with the intended expression of impatience.

"I need to apologize." I blow out a breath. "I'm sorry, Rosie. For a lot of things."

"You're sorry?" She perches her hands on her hips. "Are we really doing this now? I just got back from touring the venue for my wedding."

"Damn right we're doing this now. It's been a long time coming."

"And who's fault is that?" She fires back.

"It's mine." I tap my chest. "I'm the one to blame for this and I'm so fucking sorry."

"For what Greyson? For barging into my house in the middle of the night? For kissing me like you had any right to?" She drops her hands and takes a few steps to me. "Or are you sorry for what happened seven years ago? When you made me believe *we* actually meant something to each other? Or could be you're sorry for ghosting me? For leaving without so much as a fucking goodbye!" She shouts.

"All of it," I shout back.

She flinches at my raised voice and my hands tug at my hair.

"I'm sorry I ever made you feel like we didn't mean anything to each other. But fuck, Tilly. You were seventeen!" I shake my head. "I was leaving. You had school and plans and......"

"I wasn't jailbait, Greyson." She throws her hands out. "It wasn't like it was illegal."

"You were in high school." I glance up at the ceiling before I add. "And vulnerable. Your mom had just died. And Adam...he was my best friend and he..."

"Asked you to talk to me." She finishes. "What? You think I didn't know he asked you to see just how screwed up I was?"

My brows furrow. "How did you know that?"

She lets out a weak laugh. "I overheard you and him on the phone. After you left."

I swallow, trying to remember the conversation.

She turns to the pile of mail, reaching out to comb through the random envelopes. "You didn't spend time with me because you wanted to, you did it because he asked you to." Her voice cracks on the last word, and it echoes through my heart. I hate the pain it carries.

"He did," I admit. "He did ask me. And I had no idea…" I move towards her. "I had no idea that you would end up meaning so much to me."

Her shoulders tense before she slams a white envelope down. "You said it was a mistake."

I step up next to her. She won't look at me, but I can see her profile. "It was."

She bites down on her lip, hurt written all over that beautiful face, but I keep going. It's not what she thinks it is.

"It was a mistake to kiss you and touch you when I couldn't make you mine." I take another step closer. "I let my guard down. I was selfish and I kissed you. I kissed you because I couldn't stand the thought of anyone else getting to. I kissed you knowing I was leaving. I kissed you knowing I could never tell your brother I was falling in love with his seventeen year old sister. And it wasn't fair to you."

Her face jerks up to mine as I continue stepping towards her, rushing her until her back hits the wall. I move slowly, caging her in with my arms. "That night…." I could barely get the words out.

"I wasn't stupid, Greyson. I knew *us,* wasn't something that could happen. I mean look at me." She waves a hand over her body. "I can't compete with the kind of women you've been with. I'm plain. I'm simple……I'm *deaf.*" Her lips tremble as she turns her chin away, but I grip it gently in my fingers, turning her back towards me.

Her eyes shine, glossy from the tears she refuses to let fall.

I pinch slightly to get her attention. "What you *are* is fucking perfect."

She sucks in a deep breath, her eyes searching my face. I was already in this deep, so I let it all out.

"You deserved the world and at the time I wasn't able to give it to you." My fingers brush a piece of hair out of her face. "But I can now. And I would." I peer into her eyes, baring my soul to her in the only way I knew how. "I know you are supposed to marry him, and I know I have no right to show up and make these declarations, but these feeling are nothing new to me, Rosie. If I thought for one second, you were in love with him. That he was the love of your life, and he was the man you wanted to grow old with I would walk away." A tear falls down her cheek, so I swipe it with the pad of my thumb. "I would. Because your happiness means everything to me."

"Greyson..." she whispers.

I could feel my throat swelling with emotion. "I'm sorry." My hands cup her face. "All these years. All the distance. There hasn't been one second of any day that was not spent loving you."

I lean my forehead against hers. "I just needed you to know."

She nods, no words forming on her mouth. I place a kiss on her forehead and reach for the door.

The only thing I can do now was pray that she believes me.

CHAPTER 27

Tilly

The Past

"I'm shocked you agreed to this" I whisper with a quiet laugh.

"It's eight degrees outside. This is better than freezing my ass off watching you skate." Greyson slides down in his chair.

There's only a handful of people in the movie theater.

He hates scary movies, while I find them intriguing. I don't know if it's the adrenaline, the impulsive decisions, or how one reacts to the fight for survival. I just like it. And apparently the badass football player next to me is less than intrigued.

"Are you going to be on your phone the entire time?" I question.

He glances at me. "I'm only here for moral support."

"You're here because you're hiding from your dad," I quip.

"I'm a grown ass man. I don't hide, Rosie," he scoffs.

The movie starts up, so I sign instead of interrupting the people three rows behind us.

Then your grown ass should be able to watch this. *I sign before pointing to the screen.*

Keep it up. *He signs.* I'd hate to have to bend you over my knee for your smart mouth.

Tingles erupt between my legs at the threat.

The innocent threat because he sees me as a sibling. Not a sexual partner.

Get it together, Tills.

His signing has improved, and a warm feeling wraps around my heart at the fact he learned. For me. I let the thought go as quick as it comes. It's not healthy for me to create unrealistic situations in my head. Like the one where my brother's best friend doesn't just see me as a "little sister."

I glance over to see a text come through on his phone.

Sarah.

Jealousy burns in my stomach. He's about to be in the NFL. Famous. Women will be falling at his feet on a daily basis. Women who are...not like me.

He swipes the notification off the screen, ignoring the text, but I know he's only doing it because I'm next to him. Because contrary to what you expect most college athletes to be like, Greyson is a good guy, and he would never intentionally do anything to hurt my feelings. That doesn't mean I don't hurt them on my own. I bring most of it on myself. Letting myself get lost in a fictional world where this friendship turns into more.

You can answer you know. *I sign, motioning to his phone.*

Answer what? *He frowns.*

Your...girlfriend. *I grab some popcorn, filling my hands so I won't say something else idiotic.*

He lifts a brow and instead of signing he leans over to my ear. "If I had a girlfriend, you really think I'd be sitting in this movie theater with you? Another woman?"

I shrug a shoulder, acting like the warm breath that just bathed my skin didn't make me break out in goosebumps. Like it always does.

Lifting my hands, I sign. I don't really count, Greyson.

I expect him to laugh or have a witty come back, but he just leans in again and whispers. "You're the only one who counts."

CHAPTER 28

Tilly

I laid awake for hours last night. Greyson's words were on loop in my brain. All the words I had wanted to hear for so long. *Years.* But his timing couldn't be more terrible. I guess if you think about it, it's kind of our thing. The timing was terrible back then, and it isn't much better now. Especially as I sit here at my desk, my eyes zoned in on the diamond ring I accepted not even a week ago.

It's one of those days I needed the silence, so I left my hearing aids at home. I had no sessions today. It was a day to catch up on paperwork anyway. I needed to sort through my thoughts, my feelings, my truths. And the truth was, I wasn't in love with Blaine McKnight. I loved the idea of him. *At first.* I loved the idea of someone loving me. I knew who my heart really belonged to. Who it had always belonged to. But it wasn't just Greyson's confession that's opened my eyes.

My hand reaches up to rub my bicep. I woke to bruises painting my skin. Bruises that someone who claimed to love me put there. I never wanted to be that person. The person who gets taken advantage of. My family has always been afraid I would be due to my impaired hearing, but in this situation, it has nothing to do with it. My impaired heart was the cause of the predicament I found myself in.

I check my phone, seeing the time Blaine had texted back when he would be available for dinner. I asked him to come to my house tonight to discuss the wedding. I was surprised he agreed, but he told me he'd be there at seven PM sharp. I knew what I had to do. And it couldn't wait any longer.

The smell of garlic bread fills my cabin. I made my homemade pasta sauce and have a fresh salad in a large bowl in the middle of the table. Blaine's Audi pulls into the driveway and a wave of nervousness creeps into my body. He hadn't handled my opposition to the wedding date very well, so I was sure he wasn't going to be happy tonight. But I wanted to have a meal and talk a few things over. I wanted to be honest with him.

His knock sounds at the door, so I swipe my hands on a rag before answering. I was dressed in my casual lounge pants with an oversized sweater. I smile, greeting him with a quick kiss on the cheek before moving towards the kitchen.

"Smells good." He removes his coat. "I see you dressed for the occasion."

I take a deep breath. Had he always been this subtle with his jabs? How did I never notice?

"It's my home. I can dress how I like." I grab the spoon, stirring the marinara before moving the pan to the table.

"I guess these aren't so bad." He catches my waist as I step away. "Should be easy to get off."

His hand slides across the waistband, traveling dangerously close to where I did not want him. *Ever again.* He plants a kiss on my neck and a sick sense slithers over me.

"Dinner is ready." I slip out of his grip before he can argue.

We take our seats. I had a fire going in the fireplace and soft music playing. I was hoping to create a calm environment for when I inevitably broke things off. *For good.*

We ate in silence. When we finish our plates, he breaks the tension with a question that would change the course of this evening. "You said you wanted to discuss the wedding. Did you finally come to terms with the date?"

I swallow the last bite I have in my mouth, dabbing my napkin over my lips. "Actually." I clear my throat. "I need to be honest with you, Blaine."

He tosses his napkin on the table and gives me his attention. "Let's hear it, sweetheart."

I nervously twist the ring on my finger. "I..." I feel like I'm suffocating. Like the words were wrapping around my throat. I fought the urge to sign. He wouldn't be able to understand me anyway.

"I don't want to get married," I blurt.

His face remains neutral. No sign of emotion.

I clasp my hands together. "Did you hear me?"

He runs his thumb along his lip. "Oh, I heard you. I'm just trying to figure out what has given you the audacity."

I rare back. "Excuse me?"

"Why?" He questions.

"Why what?"

"Give me a reason you don't want to marry me? You know how many women would kill to be in your shoes?" He scoots back from the table.

"I'm just.... this happened too fast. I thought I was in a place where I was ready, but I'm not." I place my napkin next to my plate.

With shaky hands I remove the ring from my finger, placing it on the table in front of him. "I'm sorry. I never meant..."

I didn't get the words out before his arm stretches out, forcefully raking our plates and the entirety of the dinner I cooked onto the floor.

"Put that fucking ring back on your finger!" He roars.

I shoot up from the chair, jumping back as my plate of spaghetti tumbles to the floor.

"Blaine!" I scold. "That's enough!"

His strides were quick and unexpected when he steps around my chair. "You think you can leave me?"

I wasn't fast enough. The sting was immediate when he backhands me across the face. The metallic taste of blood coats my tongue as I stumble, falling over the back of the couch.

Instinctively I move my hands to mouth. "Blaine," I croak.

His eyes had the same hollow look as they did yesterday. Cold and empty. "Is this about that football player?" He laughs, loud like a maniac as I scramble to my feet.

"You really think he wants someone like you?"

I had just regained my footing when he snatches me up by my hair. I cry out in pain as he yanks me towards him. "I was willing to overlook your shortcomings." He tugs my head back, baring his teeth at me.

Bile rose in my throat, and I dug my nails into his wrists. I was sick. Sick that I let him manipulate me.

"You'll regret this." I grit out. "You think my father, or my brother will let you get away with this?"

His grip tightens. "You forget the power I hold, Tilly." He leans down, placing a wet kiss on my jaw. "Now. I'm willing to overlook this little tantrum you've thrown."

His words ignite a surge of anger, and I use my elbow, lifting it up as far as I can before I ram it into his ribs.

"Bitch," he hisses as he doubles over.

"Get out!" I shriek.

I dart over to the chest I keep next to Nelson's cage. I was an officer's daughter, and I was trained to use a weapon at a young age. I fumble the drawer open, before pulling out the pistol I keep for situations just like this.

I raise it, pointing it directly at his shocked face. "Get. The fuck. Out," I demand.

His hands raise and his expression immediately morphs from enraged to panicked. "Woah, baby. Come on." He shakes his head. "This got out of hand. I'm sorry."

"No." I move a step closer. "Leave. Now. We're done, Blaine."

His nostrils flare as he backs up.

"Tilly."

"Leave!" I scream.

He jolts but finally, turns for the door. But because he was an arrogant prick he turns, looking at me over his shoulder. "When you decide to stop being a bitch, we'll discuss this further."

"There's nothing to discuss. It's over," I snap.

"It's over when *I* say it is." His voice was full of something sinister. Something I had never experienced. "Oh, and go ahead and tell that pathetic excuse for a cop brother of yours. I'm a well know lawyer, Tilana. You're delusional if you think anything against me will stand in court." He winks. "See you soon, baby."

Then he slams the door.

And I fell to the floor.

CHAPTER 29

Greyson

I had stopped by the center this evening to talk with Dixie. She wanted to do a day camp one Saturday so we were hashing out the details. I was hoping to run into Tilly. We hadn't talked since last night when I pretty much laid out every feeling I'd kept hidden the last seven years.

"She left for the day."

I turn to the voice just as I enter Tilly's office.

Lucy stands at the end of the hall, a stack of papers in hand. "She was having Blaine over for dinner."

My fist clench at the thought. The thought of her cooking for him. Laughing and enjoying a night at home. His arms she's laying in while she watches some ridiculous horror movie. I hate them, but I'd watch every single one of them if it meant I could just sit next to her. Hold her hand. Watch her talk to the tv characters like they can actually hear her warnings.

"She wasn't herself today." Lucy chews on her lip. "She didn't even wear her hearing aids."

That got my attention. She only did that when she was overwhelmed. *Thinking*. Was she thinking about us? I grasp onto the notion like a lifeline.

"Thanks Lucy." I wave before heading out the door.

I did something I hadn't done in years. I went to the lake. To the spot that not only brought us together but tore us apart. I sat down on the rock, imagining her skating across the ice. She was so fearless. Jumping and spinning like nothing in this world could stop her. I can't count the number of YouTube videos we watched as she tried to master a new technique. It wasn't even something she wanted to do for sport. She wanted to do it for *herself*.

I let my mind travel back. Back to the night I crossed a line.

The past

I answered my phone on the second ring. "Grey."

"Rosie." I glance at the clock. It was just after ten PM.

"Did you know that flamingo's mate for life?"

I chuckle as I stretch my feet onto my coffee table. "I was not aware of that random fact."

"Well, they do." She pauses. "I think it's fascinating."

I think you're fascinating.

I close my eyes. I wasn't suppose to have these thoughts about her. These feelings. But I did and they were getting stronger and harder to control every time I talked to her.

"Is there a reason you called me about flamingos at ten o'clock at night?" I ask.

"I almost had sex tonight," she blurts.

I freeze. My entire body going rigid. The thought of someone touching her. Anyone touching her but me made me physically nauseas. I hadn't even so much as looked at another woman since we started whatever this was. Which was not my norm and I'd had to avoid constant questions from my teammates. I wouldn't dare admit I couldn't touch anyone because none of them were my best friend's sister. None of them were her.

"Almost?" My throat was dry. Scratchy.

"Almost," she repeats. "But I just...," she trials off.

"You just what?" I sit up, pressing my elbows down on my knees.

You couldn't because he wasn't me?

"I don't know." She sighs. "It just didn't feel right."

"But you wanted to?" I ask.

"Yes," she answers.

Fuck.

"But not with him."

My body relaxes, but something about her voice has me doing something reckless. I was almost two hours away at my condo in Denver.

"Where are you?" I question.

"At some house party."

"A party?" I grit my teeth. "Have you been drinking?"

"A little," she admits.

Anger hit. Hard.

"You know better," I scoff. "Did he take advantage of you?"

"What? No." She gasps. "Why are you so mad?"

Because you're drunk and you let some asshole touch you and I can't.

"I'm coming to get you." I snatch my keys from the table.

"Don't bother. I have a ride with Clayton."

"Fuck Clayton. Stay put, you better be there when I pull up."

I hang up and thumb to my app. I could see her exact location and I had an hour and a half to try to talk myself out of doing what I was about to do.

Too bad it didn't work.

I pull up to the house nestled amongst the trees in the town over from Timber Creek. The music was blasting, and the yard was full of people. I push my way through the door, searching the crowded room for her long blonde hair. It didn't take long to find it. She was perched on the stairs, next to some asshole in a cowboy hat.

The music was loud, so I opted to use my hands. Rosie, *I sign when I reach the staircase.*

Her eyes widen in surprise and the asshole I'm assuming is Clayton, tosses his arm over her shoulder.

You actually came? *She signs.*

This the guy? *I ask.*

A sheepish look flashes across her face before she stands, causing his arm to drop.

No. Let's go.

She was lying, but I chose to let it slide as she grips my hand, tugging me out the front door.

"What the hell are you doing here?" She hisses when we make it to my truck. "You have a meeting in the morning with your new coach! It's after midnight!"

She twirls around, her lips pursed and that same Timber Creek PD ball cap sitting on her head that was hot as fuck.

I couldn't think straight, obviously, or I wouldn't be here, staring at her like I might die if I don't taste her.

"Grey?" She presses when I don't respond. "You should be asleep. This meeting is important for your future."

One step. That's all it took. One step, one lazy movement of my hand and I was pulling her against me until my lips crashed into hers. A soft moan floats around us the second my tongue swipes inside her luscious mouth. I couldn't hold back the groan that erupted from my chest when her tiny hands dove into my hair. My body was tight. Wound. I had been fucking my own hand for months, picturing the same body beneath me. Picturing the sounds she'd make when I sank down into her so deep, she'd feel me for weeks.

She gasps when I crouch, picking her up by the back of the thighs. Her legs wrap around my waist, and I press her up against the door of my truck.

"Grey…" she whispers against me.

I swallow her words, before moving down to plant a kiss along her jaw, then her neck. "Yeah?"

My hips move, pressing against her center. I was rock hard and the way she withered against me told me she was just as desperate as I was.

She pulls back, lifting her hands. Touch me.

My fingers brush along her jaw, then I move then up to tangle in her hair.

"I can't. We can't." I breathe out.

Hell, we shouldn't even be kissing.

My forehead drops to hers. My breaths heavy. She shifted her hips, grazing against my aching cock.

"Fuck..." I grit out. "I'm trying really hard, Rosie. I'm sorry. I shouldn't do this."

"You know who I wanted it to be?" She whispers.

I lift my head to meet her eyes. "You." Her hands cup my face. "I just want you."

I suck air into my lungs before pressing my lips to hers again. It was a quick kiss. Not near enough for me, but I was leaving. We both knew it. We both knew I was leaving in four days. I'd be thousands of miles away. In another state with a new career that I had worked my ass off for. One that would take up every ounce of my time. And she'd be here, worrying. Wondering why I didn't have time for her. Not focusing on her dreams. I knew Tilly. I knew we had become attached, no matter how hard I tried to avoid it. I was fighting my own battle. I knew this would only make it worse. It would only hurt her when I left. It would hurt Adam if he found out. He trusted me.

The realization slams into me as I tear my mouth from hers. I drop her to her feet, taking a few steps away so I can catch my breath. Shit. I crossed a line.

She was panting, her lips swollen and her hair wild from my hands. She was beautiful. Vibrant. And had so much life ahead of her. A life that she needed to live. Here. Without me.

The light in her eyes dulls as she stares at me. Her smile fades and her hands lift. Grey?

I swallow, preparing for the words I was about to pour out. I swipe a hand over my mouth before uttering the biggest lie I'd ever told. "I'm sorry, Rosie." *I watch her shoulders drop.* "I shouldn't have done that. It was a mistake."

Her eyes cloud, but I ignore it, trying to keep the burning in my chest from catching me on fire. "Let me take you home."

"No." *She croaks.* "How could you...a mistake?" *Her voice shook.* "You feel it, Greyson. I know you do."

"Feel what?" *I open the door for her, keeping my eyes away from hers.*

"This." *She swipes a tear away.* "Us."

When I don't say anything, she shakes her head. "You kissed me. You came here."

"I know." *This is all my fault.*

If I would have just been stronger.

"Are you really going to pretend there isn't something between us?" *Tears stream down her cheeks.*

"There can't be an us, baby." *I motion to the seat.* "We both know that. Now get in."

She shakes her head again, tears steaming. "No."

"Tilly, you ready!" *A voice shouts.*

She turns, facing Clayton. She glances back at me, and the look she sends me nearly buckles my knees.

"Yeah. I'm ready," *she calls.*

She straightens her shoulders. Her shaky hands lift, and she signs something I'll never forget. I knew I'd never be good enough for you.

Then she storms away.

Taking my heart right along with her.

CHAPTER 30

Tilly

I sit in the floor, choking back tears. I was cursing myself. So disappointed in the fact I didn't see it. That I didn't see beneath the put together exterior of a man who didn't value me. I place the gun on the floor, taking in the disaster dinner that's scattered across the hardwood. With a deep breath I will myself to move. I crawl, my hands shaking as I pick up a fork. I place it on a broken plate, before I move to the next one. I had just reached for the other broken piece when a knock sounds at my door. I pause, praying who ever it is would go away. *I didn't want to be seen like this.*

I quickly stack the broke pieces when the knock comes again, followed by Greyson's voice.

No, No, No.

I can't see him. I'll break down. I'm fine. It was just a slap to the mouth. Nothing major.

I crawl over, dragging my pants through spilled marinara. My fingers grip the large pot, turning it right side up so I can scoop up the mess.

The door opens and I move quicker. Scooping up as many noodles as my hands will allow.

"Tilly.... what the..." Greyson begins, but I interrupt him.

"It's fine. Just a spill. No big deal." I turn my back to him, using the side of my hand to shovel the other shards of broken plates.

"Rosie, can you look at me?" His voice softens and he feels closer.

But I never stop. I stack the plates in the pot, then pick up the salad bowl.

He was even closer now. I could feel him right behind me. He places his hand gently on my back and I flinch, a sob trying to force its way out of my throat. I swipe at my chin. It feels wet.

"Baby." He crouches down next to me. "Look at me."

My hands still and I close my eyes. The heavy tears fall. They roll from my cheeks, down to the mixture of sauce and noodles beneath me. I finally gather the courage to look up. To let him see just how weak I feel. How embarrassed I am that I let this happen.

When I meet his eyes, his hand goes to his mouth. He roughly runs it across his chin. His eyes glance away, his jaw tensing before he looks back down at me.

"He did this?" He asks.

His voice was low. Anger vibrated with the question.

He lifts his hands because he knows it will comfort me. *Did he do this? I need you to tell me.* He asks again.

I sit back on my heels. *Yes. It was him.* I sign back.

As soon as my hands stop, I let everything out. A sob rips from my chest, and he falls to his knees, catching me before I collapse forward.

His arms circle me, embracing me into the only arms that ever made me feel truly safe.

My tears soak his shirt. I was too distraught at first to realize he had stood and began to carry me up the stairs to the bathroom. He gently sits me down on something solid, but I wouldn't let go. I was terrified he would leave.

"I'm not going anywhere." He places a kiss on my temple. "I'm just going to clean you up, ok."

I let my arms drop, hanging at my sides as he grabs the hand towel from the loop holder, then runs it under the water.

I take a breath before having the strength to glance at myself in the mirror. My hair is ratted, and blood is smudged on the side of my mouth and down my chin. I look just as horrific as I feel.

Embarrassment hits again. The fact I was sitting here, bleeding because I made a stupid choice.

"Don't do that." His voice fills the bathroom. "You have nothing to be embarrassed about. This is on him." He twists the rag. "Not you."

I wasn't sure if I was flattered that he knew me so well or irritated.

He gently raises the rag to my face, cleaning off the blood. I wince when it hits the open cut on my lip.

"Sorry," he mumbles.

"Thank you," I whisper.

He tosses the rag down, then reaches for my feet. His rough hands slip off my socks first, then he helps me slide off the countertop. I stand there as he carefully takes off each piece of clothing that was peppered with sauce or blood. I couldn't tell which at this point. I stand in a pair of boy-cut underwear and my nude bra. I had envisioned Greyson stripping my clothes off of me plenty of times, but it was never like this. Nothing about this was sexual. He was attentive. Gentle. And he makes sure the shower has steam bellowing out from the door before he faces me. His eyes stay on mine, not my uncovered body.

"Hop in." He steps around me. "Take as long as you need, I'll clean up downstairs."

"You don't have to." I rush out. "I can get it when I get out."

He pauses, then slides his hand up on my cheek, his thumb caressing my cheekbone. "Will you just let me take care of you, Rosie? Please."

With that he left me alone in the bathroom, and all I wanted was to feel his touch again.

CHAPTER 31

Greyson

I got out of the bathroom as calmly as I could. The last thing she needed was me losing my shit and raging in front of her. She was shaken up and although I wanted to hunt his ass down and show him the consequences of touching what's mine, I refrained. She *needed* me more than I needed revenge, so I got her taken care of and escaped down the stairs to allow myself a moment to calm down.

My blood was pumping, my anger at an all time high, and I was fighting against some blotchy spots in my vision that began when I was descending the stairs.

I rub me eyes before I take in the mess. I don't know exactly what happened, but judging by the scattered dishes, I have a pretty good idea. I take a few steps when I notice the gun on the floor. Pride fills my veins to know she protected herself. She knew how to use it. We'd went to the gun range countless times with Adam and Cap over the years.

I pick it up, checking the clip before I stuff it back in the drawer where she keeps it.

Twenty minutes later I had the floor clean. No remnants left of whatever happened at that dinner table. I wanted to know. I *needed* to know, but it had to be when she was ready. I wouldn't force her to talk about it.

Soft footsteps come from the staircase. Tilly appears at the bottom in some pajama pants and a hoodie. *My hoodie.* The same lime green fuzzy socks wrapped around her feet. She hated being bare foot. Had since she was little and the only material she could stand on her feet was the soft fuzz. She never wore anything else.

"Hey." I rinse my hands, using the towel to dry them off.

"Hey." She smiles timidly before glancing down at the clean floor. "Thank you." She clears her throat. "You didn't have to."

"I wanted to," I remind her.

She squints, then takes a few steps over to a spot on a wooden plank. "Dang it." She lowers, running her fingers over something I can't see. "There's a huge gouge in the floor." She curses under her breath. "Mr. Brown is going to flip."

I almost chuckle.

"You know how he is." She stands. "I mean, he's a good landlord, but he was very particular about damages when we signed the rent papers."

Walking over to her, I examine the spot. It's not even that big. "Don't worry about Mr. Brown."

Her hands go to her hips. "He's going to make me pay for that."

"No, he's not."

"And how do you know?" She lifts a brow.

"Because he doesn't own this house. I do," I confess.

Her face scrunches and she blinks in surprise. "What do you mean you do?"

"Well." I reach out, taking her by the hand to lead her to the couch. "What I mean is, six months after you signed the lease, I heard he was trying to sell."

I fall back on the couch, then tug her down next to me. "It was hard enough for you to find a rental here in town and I knew you didn't want to move back home, so I bought it." I shrug.

She stares at me. "I'm not sure I'm understanding."

I smirk. "There's not much to it, Rosie. I wanted you to have a place you felt independent. I know it's important to you to prove that not only to yourself, but your family. You needed a place that was *yours*. I bought it for you."

"But I send all my rent to the P.O. Box in town." She frowns. "You aren't even here how do…"

"Mom." I reach up, tucking a piece of wild hair behind her ear. "She handles the checks for me."

"Is that why my rent decreased?" She narrows her eyes.

"Yes. But you don't pay rent. I have a savings account set up in your name. It's all there," I add.

Her blue eyes grow wide, and I prepare myself for the outburst, or the *I can handle my own shit* speech I've gotten more than once from her mouth, but it doesn't come. I can see the emotions building along with a fresh set of tears.

Before I can open my mouth, she moves her hand, clasping it tight against mine.

"Grey…" she whispers.

"Yeah, baby?" I graze my thumb along her knuckles.

"What you said the other day…about there not being a single day that was not spent loving me…" she worries her lip. "Is that true?"

Her eyes are puffy, and her lips swollen. She's still the most beautiful thing I've ever seen.

"Do flamingo's mate for life?" I ask.

She squeezes my hand with a soft laugh. "According to Animal Planet, yes."

I watch her gaze go from our joined hands, back to my face. "Yeah, Rosie. Every word I said was true."

Her sharp intake of breath told me she needed to hear it, but it was only a small crack in the protective wall she had built up. It would take a lot more truths for me to reach the place I wanted to be.

Her heart.

CHAPTER 32

Tilly

My heart swells. It practically burst out of my chest. I still had so many questions and even though I had trained my mind to despise him, I was exhausted. I was exhausted from fighting this never ending battle, but I wasn't quite ready to wave the white flag.

"Come on," he nods his head.

We stand and I let him lead me back up the stairs and into my room. Without a word, he pulls the covers back on my bed, fluffing the pillow.

"Get moving, Rosie," he orders.

I walk past him and crawl into bed. He holds out his palm as I tug the covers up over my legs. I reach up, removing my hearing aids and lay them in his hand. He places them on the charger then cuts off the lamp. There's still a glow in the room from the tv, so I can see his body move towards the door, but he stops before he gets to the threshold. His large hand grips the door, closing it before he turns to face me.

What are you doing? I sign.

I figured he would leave. He did his part.

Staying. He moves back to the bed.

Panic swirls inside me. Is he planning on sleeping here? With me? *In here?* I ask.

He stops on the other side. *Where else?*

The couch?

I know if he gets close to me, holds me, that's it, I'm a goner. I'll fold like a lawn chair.

No. He signs.

I let out a deep breath, my eyes closing as I slump back into the pillows. Of course, he says no. He takes a few strides, then his shirt is over his head, his abs on full display. His hands go to his jeans next, his pants dropping against the floor so he's standing in a pair of navy boxer briefs. *Damn.*

My eyes flicker from his feet to his chest. I casually pull my gaze to his face, which wears a knowing grin.

Like what you see?

I roll my eyes. *Don't flatter yourself.*

Maybe he should sleep on the floor. I feel hot.

But yes. I like what I see very much.

He places a knee on the bed, crawling under the covers next to me.

I move quick, stuffing a pillow between us as a barrier. That lasts all of two seconds. With one sharp tug, he yanks it from between us, tossing it off the bed before he slides his arm across the cool sheets, dragging me over to collide with his solid chest.

He curls me tight against him, my nose buried in the crook of his neck. I inhale, breathing in his scent as his hand gently swipes my hair from my face.

I glance up, seeing his eyes on me. He taps his mouth, telling me to read his lips. I zone in, waiting for the words to fall from them. I may not be ready to give in, but his words mend another broken piece of my heart.

"He'll never touch you again. I promise."

I feel the pressure of something heavy on my waist. It takes me a second to realize that the heavy object is a very sculpted arm that belongs to the man currently spooning me. He's still asleep, his soft breath fanning at my back while said arm is wrapped around me. Our legs were intertwined, and it was as if he was determined to keep me held against him. Greyson didn't strike me as someone who cuddled, so I was surprised to find him wrapped around me this morning.

I lift his arm and slide out from underneath him. My bladder was screaming and the last thing I wanted to have was morning breath when I had a very hot NFL player in my bed.

I wanted to laugh at my own thought. It's funny I've never really saw him as that. As *famous*. Or *rich*. He's always been *Grey* to me.

I had just brushed my teeth and slapped on some moisturizer when the bathroom door opened. Greyson leans against the door frame; his dark hair tousled effortlessly on his head.

Morning. He signs.

I lift my hands. *Morning.*

The blinking of the clock behind him had me cursing. I brush past him, and to my closet.

I felt him follow and he frowns when I glance over to him.

Work. I sign quickly. *I'm late.*

He shakes his head. "You're off today."

I pull a black sweater from a hanger, reading his lips in the process. *It's Friday.*

"I talked to Dixie. Your classes are covered today." He grabs the sweater from my hand and tosses it to the side.

Deciding to make this easier, I move to my nightstand to put in my hearing aids.

I face him. "What did you tell her?"

"I told her you weren't feeling well." He sat down on the edge of my bed. "I figured you didn't want to be bombarded with questions on what happened to your lip."

I gently touch my face, tracing my lip with my finger. "Makes sense."

I had a lot to do still. I hated missing work, and I had some things that were on a deadline.

"Lucy is bringing you over the things you need. I want you to rest today." He reaches out, tugging me towards him.

I settle in between his thighs, my palms landing on his shoulders. His touch was so delicate. Like he was caressing something worth more than precious rubies.

"Do you want to talk about it?" He asks.

His fingers were on my thighs, making a soothing motion that made my cheeks blush.

I swallow before speaking. "I ended it. I told him it was over and gave back the ring." I pause, my eyes closing as I replay last night. "He got angry. He hit me. He..." I blow out a nervous breath. "He acted as if this was just me throwing a tantrum. Like he wasn't going to take no for an answer."

Greyson's hands still and he squeezes my thighs before dropping them.

"Motherfucker," he mutters.

"I'm fine, Grey." I tip his chin up with my hand.

"I'll handle him." His jaw clenches.

"Greyson." I sigh. "I don't want you to..."

"He fucked with what's mine, Rosie. He's not getting away with that." His eyes were hard and even though it wasn't pointed towards me, a spark of fear flickered in my stomach.

He must have seen it because he softens immediately. "Hey." He pulls me closer. "I'm sorry. I didn't mean to scare you."

"You didn't," I assure him.

I step away, putting some distance between us. He stayed last night because I was hurting. But now, it's back to reality. I'm not a damsel in distress anymore. I have work, I'm sure he has to get back to Texas soon. He was here when I needed him.

"So...thank you for staying." I look around the room, searching for something to do to not make this awkward. "I appreciate you helping me, but I'm sure you have things to do and need to get back to San Antonio." I pick up the sweater he discarded, then opened a dresser drawer for some pants.

I'm too busy gathering random clothes to notice he's standing and is now hovering behind me. I meet his gaze in the mirror when I raise up, hands full of clothes I probably won't even wear today.

"If you think I'm leaving you this time, you're highly mistaken."

I suck in a breath at the seriousness in his tone.

He leans down, caging me in against the dresser. "And if you open that mouth to argue, I'll find something better to do with it."

My eyes widen and he smirks. "I'll make us some breakfast."

CHAPTER 33

Tilly

Greyson disappeared downstairs, so I change my clothes and try to make myself halfway presentable. A little canceler helped cover the spot on my lip and other than the fact my scalp is a little tender, I look completely normal.

I was dressed for comfort since I was apparently working from home today. When I made it downstairs, Greyson was standing in front of Nelson's cage. He's hunched down, seemingly intrigued by my quill covered pet.

"Meet Nelson," I said as I hit the last step.

"Where the hell did you get this?" He stands up straight. "He bristled up at me."

I laugh and lean down to be eye level with him. "He's a great judge of character." I stick my finger in the cage, and his little nose taps my fingertip. "You might want to do some self reflection."

He snorts. "What did he think of your fiancé?"

"Ex-fiancé," I correct. "And Blaine never even acknowledged him."

He reaches for his coat that's laying across the counter. "I already told Dixie I'd do a volunteer day today. I got a few boys coming this morning, but there are pancakes on the stove."

"Of course." I shake my head. "You don't have to hover over me, Greyson. I'm fine. I'm sure you have more important things to deal with."

Like the articles floating around about the altercation with his father. We haven't gotten a chance to talk about that yet.

His face grows serious after he flicks the collar of his jacket. "Rosie, I don't know how to be any clearer." He steps to me, his palms land on each side of my face. "There is *nothing* more important to me than you."

I practically melted in a puddle.

"I'm not comfortable with you being alone while I'm gone. Just in case that asshole decides to show back up." He drops a kiss on my hair. "I called Camille. She's coming over."

I feel empty the second he steps away. The way he keeps dropping kisses on me was sweet, and I hate to even admit it, but I was dying for them to land on my lips. For him to just grip me in his strong hands and kiss me stupid like he did last month. But he didn't. He sets the alarm, then walks out the door.

I know what he's doing. The ball is in my hands, and he's letting me run the play.

I feel the anger radiating from every female body in my cabin.

Apparently when Greyson called Camille, she was already getting dressed to come over. She had a *feeling* last night. Some people may think we are full of it, but the twin thing is real shit. Since she knew something was up, she gathered the reinforcements. I'm now getting *the look* from three very pissed off women.

"I'm sorry he what?" Bekka gasps.

"I'm with her." Elle hikes a thumb in Bekka's direction. "What the hell did he do to you, Tilly?"

Camille scoffs. "What he did was sign a death warrant."

"Oh hell no." Elle stands next to Bekka. "Easton has a nice set of golf clubs. I can grab those." She downs the remaining liquid in her glass of lemonade I made just minutes ago.

"Adam has a bat and I think a hockey stick too." Bekka adds.

"Ok the last thing we need is you two in jail," Camille reasons.

"Your dad loves me. He wouldn't put me in jail," Bekka says.

"I don't want to drag this out. Y'all didn't see him..." I fidget with the sleeve of my sweater. "I don't want any contact with him. I'm just glad I was able to get out before we went through with the wedding."

Camille's hand lands on my arm and I reach up, giving it a squeeze. "I should have listened to you." I squeeze again.

"None of this is your fault." Her eyes fill with tears. "No man has a right to lay his hands on you. For any reason."

"We're here for whatever you need, Tills." Bekka pauses. "You know you're going to have to tell your dad and Adam."

I blow out a breath. "I know."

I don't plan on telling them about his last words. *See you soon, baby.* They'll have a freaking squad car parked at my house 24/7 or something equally over dramatic.

"And you guys were right." I push to stand. "As much as it pains me to admit that. I was ignoring the red flags and I should have listened."

"Well, taking responsibility for your fuck ups is the first step." Elle nods.

"Eloise." Cami hisses.

"What?" She shrugs.

I huff out a light laugh. "She's right."

"So...since that's over..." Bekka trails off.

I narrow my eyes. "So, what?"

"Another elephant in the room we are going to ignore?" Elle smirks.

"Greyson?" Camille questions.

I keep my face neutral. "What does he have to do with anything?"

"I don't know. Maybe the fact he was here *this morning.*" Bekka leans up from her position on the couch.

"And?" I turn, walking to the kitchen.

"And the fact he showed up at your house in the middle of the night and kissed you while Blaine was asleep." She tosses her hands up.

My eyes widen and she slaps a hand over her mouth as Elle and Camille both shout. "What?" In unison.

"I hate you," I grit out.

"Sorry," she mutters.

"When did this happen?" Camille asks.

"The night before the charity auction," I admit as I pick up a box of Vanilla Wafers.

"Oh my God. That's why you slapped him?" Elle's eyes light up like she just solved a decades long cold case.

"What slap?" Camille stomps her foot. "Why do I not know any of this?"

I groan and tilt my head back. "Look, he showed up on my door step at two in the morning. I opened, he said he needed me, pushed me against the wall then his mouth was on mine. It happened so fast and I was just..." I drop the cookie box on the counter a little too hard. "I let him ok! I'm a horrible human because I let him while Blaine was literally one floor up, sleeping in my bed."

The kitchen goes quiet. "Blaine and I hadn't labeled our relationship yet, but I still felt..."

"Guilty," Camille inserts.

"Is that why you accepted his proposal? You felt guilty?" Elle asks.

"Or was this more of a way of protecting yourself?" Bekka's tone was soft. "If you gave your heart to Blaine, someone else wouldn't be able to break it anymore?"

Her question slams into me. Was that what this was? Was I dumb enough to think attaching myself to someone else would make ten years worth of feelings disappear?

"It was your armor." Camille walks over, reaching across the island. "If you had that ring on, it protected you." She shakes her head. "Sister, there is no amount of amor you can put on to keep real love out."

"I've never told you, or Elle. How do y'all even know?" I ask.

"Seriously?" Elle laughs. "Have you not seen the way he looks at you?"

"What? With pity?" I croak. "He's a famous football player. He has women throwing themselves at him left and right. He's been pictured with numerous. He's not pining over the deaf girl in his hometown."

"Tills..." Cami starts.

I know all the things he said. I know he told me just hours ago I was the most important thing to him, but self doubt is a nasty habit to break.

"He was here this morning because he came over last night right after the incident. He stayed because he felt bad for me. My "fiancé". I use air quotes. "Had just slapped me across the face and threatened me. Of course he stayed. It was the nice thing to do."

"Nice? Where did he sleep?" Elle crosses her arms.

I hesitate, rolling my lips together. "With me."

Bekka smiles and Camille holds her hand to her heart like I just made some sort of life changing public declaration.

"Nothing is going on. I literally just dumped my fiancé less than twenty-four hours ago." I roll my eyes.

"I don't give a shit if you dumped him two hours ago. Greyson Roy has it *bad* for you." Elle climbs off the couch. "He literally flew from a different state the second he heard you were engaged."

Bekka and Camille both swoon like a couple of teenagers.

"He helped me. We have history. He's Adam's best friend." I close eyes. "We're friends..." I trail off.

"I saw the look on his face, Tilly." Elle meets my eyes. "He asked me point blank if you were in love with Blaine."

I frown. "When?"

"The morning, he got here. And you know how I know that man loves you?" She uncrosses her arms. "If I would have said yes. That you were in love and happy, he would have let you be. He would have spent the rest of his life miserable, as long as *you* were happy."

"Damn," Bekka mumbles.

"What she said," Camille adds.

"I'm scared." I let the truth fall from my lips. "He broke my heart once; I'd be stupid to let him do it again."

"But what if he doesn't?" Elle questions.

What if he doesn't? That's a terrifying question.

CHAPTER 34

Greyson

I spent the morning talking about work ethic, physical and mental toughness, along with what the dreams were of a group of boys who weren't much bigger than my left thigh. But the enthusiasm and attitude from each one has the idea I've had brewing, seem like more of a reality.

Adam had called, but I let it go to voicemail. If I talked to him, I'd let him know what a piece of shit his sister's ex-fiancé was and I wanted to let Tilly be the one to tell him. Although it wasn't my place, the possessive side of me wanted to take matters into my own hands. To tell Adam, her father, and whoever else wanted to join in on the revenge I planned to shell out. *Which I would.* I had her engagement ring burning a hole in my pocket. I found it amongst the dinner that was scattered on the floor. I plan to return if myself and make sure he understands that if he so much as breathes in her direction, he's a dead man.

When I pull up to my house, my brother's car is in the drive. He must be visiting mom. I come through the door to hear my mom's laughter and June's giggles. I had three important women in my life, and two of them were in the living room.

I sent Easton a tilt of my chin. "Hey."

He nods back just as June screams. Her little legs charge to me, and I lift her up, tossing her up in the air before I catch her.

She shrieks and her little arms squeeze around my neck. "I'm sleeping over with CiCi."

"Is that so?" I tickle her sides. "Why wasn't I invited?"

"Unky Grey!!" She squirms until I sit her down. "No boys allowed!"

"Sorry, Greyson. She's right. Girls' night only." My mom approaches, plastering a kiss on my cheek.

"Mom."

"What?" She wipes my cheek with her thumb. "Sorry."

Easton motions towards the kitchen, so I leave the girls to continue their wild night of fun.

"You got plans tonight?" He asks.

You mean besides crawling in bed next to Tilly? "Not really." I clear my throat. "What's up?"

"I thought we'd have a get together. We're not kid free that often." He chuckles. "Jace and Camille are coming around seven. Thought maybe you'd want to come." He pauses, glancing into the living room. "Maybe Tilly can come."

"We'll be there." I slap him on the shoulder.

"We?" He lifts a brow. "Together?"

"Look, some shit went down with Blaine." My jaw clenches. "She ended it last night."

"Oh, wow. Didn't think she'd do it this soon."

"What do you mean?" I ask.

"I just figured she wouldn't cave this fast." He shrugs. "You won her over quick."

"It's not like that." I run a hand through my hair. "I mean...we talked, and I told her how I felt."

"But?"

"I'm telling you this as my brother, not a cop." I lean against the cabinet. "He put his hands on her."

Easton's eyes harden. "He what?"

"She was a mess last night when I got there. He had torn up the kitchen. Hit her in the face."

"Fuck..." he curses.

"She's planning on telling Adam and Cap. She just needed to get herself together. She said he didn't seem like he was going to take no for an answer." I shift off the cabinet. "I don't want her being alone."

"I'm sorry, man." Easton meets my eyes. "What are you going to do?"

I level him with a look. "I'm going to protect my girl."

CHAPTER 35

Tilly

I hang up the phone, and slouch against the couch. I called my dad to let him know that I had ended it with Blaine. I left out all the details. He didn't need to know. He would probably want to press charges, but all I wanted was to put him behind me. I told him the truth. I felt I dove in head first, and realized I'd made a mistake. He was understanding and told me how much he loved me and all he wanted was for me to be happy. Richard Harper was my hero. He loved my mother so fiercely it almost seemed impossible that I'd ever find someone to love me that way.

The girls had stayed most of the morning, but left right after lunch. Camille had to check with Greyson which ticked me off a little. Like he was now in charge of my life. I'm in charge of my independence. He should know how I feel about that by now.

I scoff to myself just as a knock sounds at my door, so I pull myself up off the couch to answer. Lucy stands with a bright smile, a folder, and a cup of coffee in hand.

"Afternoon!" She chirps, but her brightness dissolves when she catches a glimpse of my lip. "What happened to you?"

I reach up to touch my lip and roll my eyes playfully. "Wire hanger one, Tilly, zero "

She laughs. "Gotcha. Been there."

Thankfully she didn't press any further, but her expression didn't show she was completely convinced. "Here's everything you need. Sorry, I was hoping to swing by this morning, but it was a little hectic today." She hands me the folder. "And I figured you'd need this." She holds out the cup.

"Thank God," I gasp.

"Anything else?" She asks.

I take a sip. "I think I'm good."

"Ok. You need anything just call. I'll be at the office all day and you know I'm just a few houses down."

"Thanks, Luce," I appreciate it.

She left with a wave. Lucy lived in the Fuller's guest cabin just down the road. It came in handy when either of us needed to carpool and she popped in at least once a week, usually to bring us dinner.

With a sigh, I drop the folder on the table, sit down, and get to work. The sooner this is done, the sooner I could figure out what the heck I was going to do about Greyson Roy.

It was nearing six thirty when I finished up. I hadn't heard from Greyson all day. I knew he was busy and frankly he didn't owe me anything. I mean, he owed the apology, but other than that, we were still in unfamiliar territory.

My phone buzzes on the table and I quickly swipe it, hoping to see Greyson's name flashing across my screen. My stomach sours when I read another name instead.

Blaine.

I silence it, just as I hear the front door open.

Greyson strides in and I perch my hands on my hips. "That door was locked."

He smirks, waving a silver key. "I own this place, Rosie. Remember?"

"So, you just don't even knock anymore?"

His steps close the distance between us. "I slept in your bed with your ass pressed against my cock all night. We're past knocking, don't you think?"

My jaw hangs open, but he just keeps walking past me, and into the small bathroom off the living room.

It takes a moment for me to get my mind off the way he said *cock.* Now I was picturing it....picturing me...

The toilet flushes and I blink. He steps out. "We're going to Easton and Elle's tonight."

"For what?" My brows scrunch.

"Dinner."

"Now?" I ask.

"Yes, now."

"Greyson! A little heads up. I need to change." I motion to my old sweats. "I look homeless. The split lip isn't helping either."

"You could wear a paper sack and still be the most beautiful girl in the entire room." He drops down on one of the dining room chairs and crosses his arms. "But if you're putting on jeans, wear the ones with the blue pockets. They make your ass look hot as fuck."

I snort. "I've literally had those for years. Like since high school."

His eyes meet mine. "I know."

Did he just admit to checking out my ass for years?

"Get moving, Rosie," he orders.

"You sure are bossy," I huff out.

I jog up the stairs, slip off my sweats and head straight to my closet. I knew exactly what I was wearing tonight.

The fire was going in the back yard, and the guys were huddled around the grill. My brother and Bekka were on the way and nerves crept up my spine. I hadn't told him about the break up yet and when he saw my lip he was most likely going to lose his shit. He's *very* sensitive to violence against women. Especially after Bekka's situation.

"Stop worrying." Camille appears next to me. "Everything is going to be fine."

I lean my head on her shoulder. "I know, you just know how he is."

"He loves you, Till. We all do and we're all angry for what he did." She wraps an arm around me.

"Thanks Cami."

Elle's laugh echoes around the yard as Easton tosses her over his shoulder. I swear those two couldn't be more perfect for each other. Their road has been just about as smooth as mine and Greyson's. A lot of lost time and regrets. I'm just not sure if our road leads to the same place as theirs.

Jace and Rex join the circle, plopping down in the lawn chairs around the fire.

"Hey trouble maker." Rex smirks, then tugs at my waist.

"Hey." I toss my arm over his shoulder as I fall onto his lap.

I'd known Rex since grade school. He was like the perfect male best friend. Protective, but also the one to be a partner in crime when needed. We'd broken the rules together many times.

"I hear you're back on the market?" He lifts a brow.

I glance over at Jace, and he shrugs.

"You heard right."

He leans in to whisper, but still speaks so Jace can hear. "Camille broke my heart when she chose Jace. It could use some mending."

I laugh and slap his shoulder. "You wish, Rexy."

"Hey, I didn't guard your cabin this afternoon for nothing," he quips.

"You what?" I gasp.

"Oh yeah, that was Greyson's compromise when we all had to leave." Camille smiles.

I feel his eyes before I even turn my head. Greyson is stalking towards us, and he clearly isn't happy.

Rex squeezes my thigh. "You might want to get up, Tilly. He's a big motherfucker and I got a Tinder date tomorrow."

I laugh again and stand just as Greyson approaches with a scowl on his face.

"Hey man. Killer season," Rex greets.

"Shut up, Rex," Greyson barks and Jace chuckles.

I give a dramatic display of innocence before blinking up at him. "Hey."

His hand reaches out to curl around the small of my back. His heavy palm tugs me to him, causing my breath to hitch, but the moment is interrupted by my phone buzzing in my back pocket.

I didn't move.

"You can answer."

I shake my head. "No, it's fine."

His eyes narrow on me.

Blaine had called three more times since we left and I was afraid. I didn't want Greyson to find out and end up doing anything he would regret.

We stare at each other, and just as he opens his mouth to speak, I hear my brother's voice. I quickly step away, putting a reasonable amount of distance between us. Greyson clears his throat as Adam joins the group.

He shakes Rex's hand, then Greyson's before his eyes land on mine. He freezes, his gaze landing on my lip.

Anxiously I pull it between my teeth and turn my face away.

"Tilana." His voice is serious. I hated when he went into *authority mode.* And used my government name.

I face him, holding my chin high. His hands were practically shaking, but Bekka steps up, sliding one of her hands into his.

"Maybe you two should talk in private," she whispers.

He nods and she kisses his cheek before he starts towards the side of the house.

I let out a deep breath as he turns to walk away.

Greyson lifts his hands. *You good?*

His concern made my chest squeeze. *I'm good.*

CHAPTER 36

Greyson

I watch Adam and Tilly from across the yard. I knew her, but I also knew my best friend. Adam could be a hot head when it came to the people he cared about. He almost lost his badge when shit went down with Bekka a few years back. I could tell by his body language she told him everything and she swipes at her face a few times before he hugs her.

I hated what happened. I hated I couldn't stop it.

You could have if you hadn't waited seven years.

"I can see the wheels turning." My brother steps up next to me. "And it's not your fault."

"If I would have been here..."

"Grey, it's a shitty situation. Neither you nor her are to blame," he cut in.

I keep my gaze on her, taking a drink of the beer I have in my hand.

They finally part and Adam disappears inside the house. I'm sure to get control and Tilly wanders back to the fire where the girls sit. I blow out a breath before I start towards the house. I've needed to have this conversation with my best friend for a long time and now was as good as ever to get it over with.

I walk into the kitchen. Adam had his hands planted against the counter. His head hanging low.

"I want to kill him, Grey." His voice was dark.

"You and me both." I walk over next to him, taking a seat on one of the barstools.

I let the silence linger a moment before I speak. "I need to tell you something. I know you're pissed right now, but it needs to be said and I'm going to ask you to not to lose your shit until I explain."

"Explain what?" He lifts his head.

"Well....me and Tilly..."

"You and Tilly what?" He questions gruffly.

"I just want you to know I tried like hell, Adam. I really did," I say as I focus my eyes on the stove across the kitchen.

"What exactly are you trying to tell me, Greyson?" His voice sounds halfway amused now.

"I wanted to explain why I'm here and that I'm...." I trail off, trying to get the words out. It may change everything.

"That you're in love with my sister?" He finishes.

My eyes darted to his. "You know?"

He barks out an exhausted laugh. "Of course, I fucking know." He pushes away from the counter and jerks out a stool. He sits down and rests his elbows on the counter. "I'd have to be the most worthless cop on the force if I didn't know."

I lift a shoulder. "I honestly didn't think I was being that obvious."

Relief washes over me that he wasn't bashing in my face, but I also hadn't told him she was seventeen when it happened.

"I uh…" I rub my palms together, nervously. "I've loved her for a long time, Adam."

"I know," he says quietly. "And I know that when you left it was miserable for both of you, but you did the right thing."

"How do you know all of this?" I ask in confusion.

"Grey, do you really think I didn't keep tabs on her? She was a loose cannon. I knew she was going somewhere after school most days, so I followed her for about a week." He faces me. "She was meeting *you.*"

"I talked to her like you asked me to…and things just…." I lift my hands up and drop them back to the counter.

"Developed?" He asks.

"Yeah." I reach up, scratching my jaw. "It scared the shit out of me." I admit. "She was young…and your sister." I point out. "I was leaving." I add.

He nods. "And you let her grow up. She needed that."

"I know how it looks. That I just left her behind and went on with my life, but I never forgot her. Ever." My voice was damn near hoarse. "When I found out she was marrying that prick, it…." I clench my fists. "It wasn't supposed to be that way."

"You know you weren't very subtle," he deadpans. "Right after you left." He lifts a brow.

Yeah. I hadn't told her about that.

"It pretty much solidified my suspicions when you spent the majority of your sign on bonus for her new hearing aids."

"What?" A voice echos from behind us.

We both spin around to see Tilly standing in the doorway. "You ......you bought me the new hearing aids?" She asks, her voice wobbles with emotion.

"You needed them," I stated.

"I'm going to be outside." Adam slaps me on the back. "I shouldn't have to give you the speech."

I chuckle. "Nah, man. I'm good."

He leaves the room and Tilly slowly crosses over to me. "I thought insurance paid for them. That's what dad told me."

"I asked them not to tell you. I didn't want recognition, Rosie. I wanted you to have what you needed. To take care of you even when I couldn't be here."

She stops in front of me, and I land my hands on her hips, positioning her between my legs.

"You did that for me?" She questions.

It kills me that she doesn't think I cared about her enough. That it was such a foreign concept.

"I would do anything for you, Tilly Harper. You name it. It's yours." My hands slide around to the back of her jeans, and I position my hands in her back pockets.

I wasn't lying when I said these jeans made her ass look good. Her arms link around my neck and I brush my nose against hers. I keep our noses touching, but I don't make a move.

I was giving that choice to her. Letting her take the lead on where she wants this to go. The kitchen is quiet. So quiet I can almost hear the pounding of her heart. She inches closer. Her body slowly melting into mine.

"Are you going to kiss me or what, pretty boy?" She murmurs.

I smile, then my hand snakes up her spine to grip her neck. "If that's what you want."

"Yes," she breathes out.

My lips hit hers. She moans, and I slide my hand up farther, tangling it in her hair so I can angle her face where I want her. My tongue plunges, licking and tasting her like it was my lifeline. The palm that was still snug in her pocket, squeezes which earns me another moan as she pulls closer. I slow the kiss, pulling away slightly to see her face. I would give anything to take this further, but at the moment we are in Easton's kitchen, and I doubt he wants her bare ass on his countertop. Add in the fact she was assaulted just yesterday. I needed to tread carefully. Be sure she knew what she was doing.

"What's wrong?" She frowns.

"Nothing's wrong, baby. Let's just slow down." I kiss her again, but she steps away.

"Don't do that to me," she scoffs.

"Do what?"

"Coddle me." She crosses her arms.

"I'm not coddling you." I stand.

"Really? So, you're telling me if you had your tongue down one of your usual's throats, you'd tell them to 'slow down'." She cocks a hip out.

"I'm not sure why you want to bring up me and other women. What I did with other women is different."

It was. It's completely different.

"Different," she repeats, then shakes her head.

She taps her foot a few times which is her tell she's about to release her fury.

Then she lets loose. "I don't want to be treated like a glass doll, or something you have to tiptoe around." She steps to me, pointing a finger at my chest. "I will not be seen as the deaf girl, and I refuse to be seen as the girl who got beat up by her fiancé." Her nostrils flair. "Especially by you. So, I want you to do whatever you would do to someone you wanted to take home, Greyson."

I grip her hand in mine. "You don't want what I had with them."

"And why not?" She tilts her head, her eyes flaring.

"You don't want a meaningless hookup. Because that's exactly what it was. I never even got a name half of the time and the other half I couldn't even stand to look at them. I never looked at their faces because the only face I wanted to see was yours."

Her eyes widen and she tries to step back, but I pull her closer.

"You want more and so do I. So, when I finally make you mine, and believe me, it's going to happen. It won't even be close to what I had with them."

She swallows thickly, her eyes bouncing between my mine.

"Okay," she says quietly.

"Okay," I repeat.

I take her hand, winding our fingers together. "Let's get out of here."

We're driving down the road, a country song playing in the background that's hitting a little too close to home.

"Can I ask you a question?" She's looking out the window of my truck.

"Fire away." I rest my hand on top of the steering wheel.

"Why didn't you say goodbye?" Her question makes my breath pinch. It's almost painful.

"I waited; you know." She peers down at her hands that are in her lap. "I waited and you never showed."

Thankfully we're pulling in her driveway, so I park the truck. I remember that night. She's asked me to meet her at the lake. I was leaving the next morning, and we hadn't spoken since the kiss. Since I screwed up.

"It had nothing to do with you, Rosie." I turn in my seat to face her. "Adam showed up at the house and wanted to have one last night out. East was there, Rex, and a few other guys. I went and planned to cut out early, but I had a hard time trying to make up an excuse to leave." She nods her head. "I couldn't really tell him I needed to leave to meet you."

"I get it," she says quietly.

"Doesn't make it right." The music still plays as the heavy emotion settles in the truck. "I again, did the selfish thing. I had my pity party. I got wasted. I figured if I got drunk it would numb me just enough that when I got on that plane it wouldn't feel like I was being ripped apart."

"I thought you forgot me." She finally turns her pretty face to me. "I didn't want to keep you from leaving, Grey. I just wanted you to take a small part of me with you."

My fingers lift and I run my thumb along her jaw. "I did. Not just a piece. All of you. You were always with me, Rosie."

A tear slips down her cheek and it lands on my skin. "You were with me too."

Her words give me the hope I had been needing since I arrived.

Her phone buzzes again. I had heard it multiple times tonight, so before she could get to it, I reach behind her and slide it out of her pocket.

"Grey." She lunges for it, but I already see it.

Anger builds in my chest as I read a slew of text messages from her ex-fiancé.

Blaine: answer your fucking phone.

Blaine: ANSWER me bitch.

Blaine: This isn't over. Don't make me come out there. You won't like what happens. I can promise you that.

Her face is pure panic. I calmly lay the phone in her hand. "Go inside."

"What?" She looks confused. "Where are you going?"

"Just get inside and wait for me." I lean across the seat, opening the door. "I'll be back."

She hesitates, her eyes pleading with me to not do what I'm about to do, but she gives in, closing the door behind her before she goes to the house. I watch her close the door then I shift into reverse.

Blaine McKnight fucked up. Big time.

CHAPTER 37

Tilly

I've been pacing for so long I thought I had rubbed off all the fuzz on my favorite socks. Greyson left four and a half hours ago. I hadn't heard from him. I wasn't one hundred percent sure where he went, but I had a good idea. I wasn't sure how he even knew where Blaine lived, but I didn't put nothing past him these days.

Headlights shine through my window as I make the thousandth trip from my dining room to kitchen. I hold my breath as they shut off, wrapping my arms around my waist. It seems like hours had passed when the knob jiggles, then Greyson steps in.

I sigh in relief when he closes the door and faces me.

I drop my arms. "Where have you been? I've been worried sick."

He tugs off his coat, and that's when I see his right hand. A few of his knuckles were scrapped, the skin red where he had obviously hit something.

"Grey…" I whisper.

"I'm fine." He takes a few strides towards me, before he scoops me up by my waist.

My arms immediately wind around him, and he buries his face in my neck. I feel a few deep breaths against me before he kisses my pulse point, then my jaw, before meeting my lips. I kiss him once, then pull back so I can see his eyes.

"What happened? Where were you?"

He leans his forehead against mine. "I delivered your engagement ring back to its owner."

My head shot up. "What?"

"Blaine won't be a problem anymore," he adds.

"Are you…" I trail off. "How did you even know where he lived?"

"Baxter. He can hack anything."

"You have a teammate that's a hacker?"

What kind of men are they hiring?

His arms tighten around me. "I handled it." He searches my face. "Do you trust me?"

I nod. "Yes. Yes, I trust you."

"Good." He drops me to my feet.

Then his voice lowers. "Take off your pants."

"My…" I started to question, but his expression makes my words fall flat.

"Pants. Off."

Holy shit. This is happening. Right now.

I lick my lips, my hands moving to the button. I flick it open as my heart pounds in my chest. Slowly I slide my jeans to the floor as he tracks every move.

I stand up straight, my shoulders back as I let my eyes lock with his.

His eyes hover, lust clouding the gold specks.

"Shirt," he commands next.

I grip the hem, yanking it over my head. I wore only a matching black bra and panty set. I could hear the rumble in his chest as his eyes rake over me.

His hands lift up to sign. *Bra.*

I reach behind me, unhooking the snaps. I let it fall to the floor. My nipples peak when the cool air hits them and he traces his tongue along his bottom lip.

Panties. He signs next.

I obey again, hooking my fingers in the fabric before I slide them down my legs. I stand naked in front of Greyson Roy. Bare. Exposed. And I had never felt more confident in my life. His chest is rising with heavy breaths and when I lean down to touch my socks, he holds up a hand.

"Leave them."

I bite my lip, holding back a grin as I sign. *I didn't know socks are what do it for you.*

He takes a predatory step to me. "*You* do it for me, Rosie."

The rasp in his voice has me clenching my thighs.

He kicks the chair out from the end of the dining table, then scoops me up in one motion.

He plants me on the wooden tabletop, then drags the chair back to the head of the table. He sits, putting him eye level my center. My knees clamp together as I settle on my palms behind me.

His rough hands run up my thighs. "Spread, baby."

I shiver as I slowly drop them open, being as vulnerable as I've ever been with a man. He lands a kiss on the inside of my knee, then glides his palm up under me, bringing me closer to his mouth.

"You know how long I've waited to do this?" He asks.

My throat is dry, and I claw, searching for the edge of the table to hold me steady. He was so close, yet so far away and the anticipation of what he could do was killing me. I knew in my bones by the end of this I would completely belong to him. *In every way.*

"A long fucking time," he mutters.

As soon as the words left his mouth, I felt the smooth swipe of his tongue. My knees drop even further, and I tilt my head back on a gasp.

He hums before asking, "You know what you taste like, Rosie?" His tongue slid lazily through my center again. "You taste like, *mine.*"

Chapter 38

Greyson

Tilly's back arches off the table as soon as my tongue touches her again. I was both rock hard and pissed off at the fact Blaine fucking McKnight got to have her. That he got to taste her. Touch her.

I'm pretty sure he got the message after I left his condo tonight. I gave him the ring, a bloody nose, and a few more punches to drive home that if he *ever* comes near my girl again, it will be the last thing he does.

My palm presses down on her stomach, holding her against the table as I ravish her. My plan was to erase the last memory she had of this table. I planned for her to blush from now on anytime she even looked at it.

"Grey..." she groans as she reaches down, frantically tugging on my hair.

She yanks as she works her hips against me, placing my lips exactly where she wants them. Her smooth legs start to quiver, so I slowly add two fingers, curling them up as they slip inside her heat. She's tight, and the thought makes my cock pulse against the zipper of my jeans.

Her cries echo through the cabin as she rides my face. I move the hand that's under her, tracing the curve of her hip all the way up to her breast.

Her nipples are hard, and apparently sensitive because when I pinch one between my fingers, I can feel her grip the two fingers that are still lodged inside her.

Her hands leave my hair, balling into fists as he slams them down. "Grey..." she moans just before I clamp down on her, sucking that spot I know will have her crying my name over and over.

Which she does, until every last drop is on my tongue. When she finally relaxes, I rise from my chair. Her blonde hair is splayed out across the dark wood, her eyes heavy, and her body spread out. *Just for me.* I reach behind me, yanking my shirt over my head. It hits the floor, then my pants. I had my jeans and briefs off in less than three seconds and my aching cock in my hand.

I stroke myself as I run my hand up her stomach, then in between her breast. They were perfect, and I tweak one of her nipples again as I line myself up.

"You ready for this, Rosie?" I ask.

She nods.

"Words, baby." I roll the other nipple between my fingers.

"Yes. Please," she breathes out.

"Since you said please." I trace my tip along her slit.

"You're mine. All of you." I press forward, sliding just the tip of my cock inside her.

"Yes."

"Yes, what?" I slide in a little further.

"I'm yours," she moans.

I thrust forward, shoving her up the table as I bury myself inside her. She screams, a painful yelp that has me freezing.

"Tilly," I grit out.

Her legs catch around me. "I'm fine," she croaks.

I keep still, the ache growing as I tilt her chin to me. "Breathe."

She bites her lip, her legs tightening around me. "You're just......big," she whispers.

I go to slide out of her, I don't want to hurt her, but she clenches my waist with her legs. "Don't even think about it." Her eyes narrow. "I just want to be treated like any other girl."

My thumb traces her jaw with reverence as I peer down at her pretty face. "But you're not just any other girl, Rosie. You're *my* girl."

"Then act like it," she challenges.

"You want this right here? Like this?" I ask.

"I want you, Greyson. I don't need a fluffy bed and half ass effort." She uses her heels to press my hips deeper.

"You know I don't do anything half ass." I smirk right as my lips drop, meeting hers.

I pull back a fraction, just to slide back in. The realization that I will be the last man that will *ever* have her this way has me slamming into her on the next thrust. I hover over her body as I pump into her. Long, hard strokes as she begins to relax and dig her fingernails into my skin. She meets my hips with urgency, her legs still locked the base of my spine. With a lift of my head, my eyes meet hers and I never look away. I stare into those blue irises. This wasn't like any other hookup. This was deeper. This was years of hurt, regret, lust, and unresolved feelings, all wrapped into one moment. She was mine. She always had been.

Her lip's part and I feel her tense. "Grey, I'm close..."

"Rosie...."

I lean down, flickering her nipple with my tongue, causing her to cry out louder as I pump into her one last time, shoving as deep as I can go as I release inside of her. The roar that erupted from my chest damn near rattled the windows. I shove my face in the crook of her neck, where I can inhale her sweet scent before dropping a kiss on her throat. Our bodies instantly relax, and her fingers run mindlessly through my hair as I rest my head on her chest. I could feel the beat of her heart, her erratic breaths, and the sticky sweat that coated her skin.

I lean up, bracing myself on my elbows above her. She carefully runs her thumb over the scar on my eyebrow and said five words that made every single day away, every single obstacle we had went through to get here, worth it.

"I love you, Greyson Roy."

CHAPTER 39

Tilly

I said the words that have been dying to burst from my heart for the last seven years. He smiles, dropping his forehead to meet mine.

"I love you, baby. You have no idea how much I love you."

He kisses my temple.

"I don't think I ever apologized for that." I point to his eyebrow. "Sorry." I smirk.

"No, you're not," he muses.

In my defense, I had no idea he was on the other side of the door. *The door to my bedroom.* It was his own fault really. He shouldn't have been eavesdropping like a creeper.

I let my arms thud against the table. I could barely move. I don't think I've had an orgasm that intense...ever. And never more than one. Blaine wasn't really the type to hand out anything. He took and that was just how it was. *How I thought it was supposed to go.*

Grey climbs off the table before offering me his hand.

"Come on." He picks me up again and I let out a shriek as he hauls us both upstairs. *Naked.*

It's funny how such a broody man like him can be so gentle. The way he tenderly sits me on my feet, then flips on the shower. With a goofy smile, I face the mirror, noticing how thoroughly happy I look. My skin is bright, my eyes glowing. and the smile on my face is beginning to hurt as it grows. I pluck out my hearing aids, laying them on the counter and slip off my socks he insisted I keep on, before I join Greyson in the shower. His large frame takes up most of the space, but I don't mind. I had nothing to complain about in this moment. I never really got to just *look* at him. My eyes trail down the muscles in his shoulders, down his biceps, along his delicious abs, then down his thick thighs. I felt the heat in my core radiate through me when his cock twitches. I dart my gaze to his face as he runs his head under the spray. When his head tilts forward, he notices I've stepped in. He shifts over, tugging me under the water next to him.

You alight? He signs. *Did I hurt you?*

I laugh at the worry on his face.

No. I feel very satisfied.

We could have gone slower. His eyes caress me.

It would have hurt either way. I lift a shoulder. *I don't want gentle, Grey.*

He grins then snatches up a bottle of my shower gel. The liquid squeezes onto his hand, then he pauses, leaning down to smell the scent.

What? I ask.

He turns the bottle to read the name.

A thousand wishes? I question. *It's my favorite.*

He places the bottle back.

That smell. He points at me. *I smelled it the night I kissed you.*

Which time? I lift a brow.

He gives me a pointed look. *The first time.* He lathers the soap in his hands. *I've never forgot it.*

I feel myself blush. The fact he remembers my scent from seven years ago. *Gah, what is he doing to me?* I feel like a pile of mush when he says things like that.

I was too busy blushing, to notice he had moved. I startle when his palms graze along my arms. He takes the time to massage the soap along my arms before he's moving to my stomach, down my legs, then to my back. He spins me around and I plant my hands along the cold tile wall as he works the soap down my back. I've never felt anything as good as when his hands are on me.

He steps closer, pressing his wet chest against me. There's no way I can miss the steel rod against my lower back. I arch back into him when I feel feather light kisses along the back of my neck. Turning to face him, I lean back against the wall. I don't want to ruin the moment, but a question has been burning in my mind for weeks.

That night before the charity auction. I sign then swipe some water from my eyes. *Why did you come to me?*

He uses his thumbs to clear the water trickling down my cheek, then turns off the spray.

Let's talk out there. He signs.

I follow as he steps out. After wrapping a towel around himself and then me, he leads me to my bed, positioning the pillows where I can rest against them.

I slip my hearing aids back in before I settle on the mattress, my legs crossing as I face him.

His hand reaches for mine, running his thumb over my knuckles. "I'm retiring."

"Retiring? Already?" I was confused. Greyson loved football more than anything. It was his dream. A dream he achieved and excelled at. Something I thought he would do until he physically couldn't anymore.

"I'm kind of in a spot where I have to." He holds up a hand. "One sec."

He jogs out of the room but is back a few seconds later with his phone in hand.

He thumbs a few apps then hands it to me. My heart sinks when I see scans. *Brain scans.*

"Grey..." I look up at him. "What is this?"

"Doc says I've had too many concussions." He swipes the screen. "I've been having some symptoms since the last one earlier this season and he said if I didn't walk away now, it wouldn't be too surprising if I ended up with CTE."

I can feel the tears fill my eyes as I read through a bunch of words I don't understand.

"Hey." He tilts my chin. "Baby don't cry. I'm ok."

"What symptoms?" I move to the next page.

"I've had some dizziness, and some confusion at times." He scratches a spot on his jaw. "I've experienced a couple moments where I've lost time."

Lost time.

"Like blackout?" I glance back up at him.

"Yeah, I guess. It hasn't happened but a couple of times. You don't need to worry."

"I always worry about you." I hand him the phone back.

My nerves are now back to being wound like a massive ball of yarn.

"I had just gotten the news from my doctor that day before I flew out here." He lifts a shoulder. "I just needed some form of peace. To feel.... you."

I pick up his hand, intertwining our fingers. "So, what does this mean?"

"It means my football career has come to an end. I talked with coach yesterday. We had a zoom meeting. I haven't decided when to announce yet."

We haven't really talked about what happens now. Or what this between us even is.

"And how do you feel about that?"

He brings my hand up, resting it against his lips for a second before he drops it. "I think I'm ready to move to the next stage in my life."

I chew on my lip. "What happens now? Us I mean? I mean, you live in Texas."

"Not anymore." He drags me across the comforter, arranging my legs to straddle him. "I'm moving back. I own a house here you know."

I roll my eyes.

"I hear my tenant is a real pain in the ass, though. She doesn't like to be taken care of. Has a wild rodent as a pet and likes horror movies."

"She sounds like a badass," I quip.

He smiles, nipping at my lip when I lean in to kiss him. "She is." He kisses me long and deep before whispering. "And I'm so fucking in love with her."

CHAPTER 40

Tilly

Something warm and wet hits my skin. I squirm, blinking my eyes open, to find Greyson's mouth on my nipple. His tongue teases the sensitive bud, and I hum a sleepy approval. My body was exhausted in the best way. I lost count of how many times he pulled an orgasm from me last night and the sun was starting to come up when we finally drifted off to sleep.

His teeth graze me, sparking a feeling straight to my core. I let my eyes fall closed to hone in on the feeling, before I open them again.

Morning, baby. He signs.

Morning. I can already feel the heat in my cheeks. I'm not sure why I'm feeling bashful. The man had devoured every inch of me over the last six hours.

His fingers dance down my stomach, heading to where I was already throbbing just by one swirl of his tongue.

He pauses to sign. *You wet for me, Rosie?*

Why don't you find out. I move my hands before reaching out to run one through his dark strands.

His lips move, but I'm not able to read them before he's scooting down the mattress. I gladly open my legs, allowing him to nestle between them. His hot breath fans across me and I grip the sheet like a vice, waiting for my toes to curl.

He shifts an inch, then freezes. I glance down, just as he curses and pushes up to his knees.

What is it? I ask as I sit up.

Someone is at the door. He steps off the bed.

I quickly scoot to the edge, grabbing my hearing aids from the charger. I tug on my pajama pants and a random sweater, then head for the door.

"Wait for me." Greyson slides his leg into his jeans.

"Grey, it's fine. It's probably my sister." I wave him off and trot down the stairs.

The pounding comes again, so I rush over, yanking open the door. I didn't know what time it was, but I knew we had slept in. I squint as I take in my brother and Easton standing in their uniforms on my front porch.

"Adam?" I pull open the door. "What are y'all doing here. Everything ok?"

His face is neutral, but he steps past me, and Easton follows. Both were unusually quiet. Adam glances around the room, then faces me.

"Is Grey here?" He asks.

"I'm right here." Greyson comes down the stairs, tugging a t-shirt over his head.

"What's going on?" He asks.

"Why don't you sit down, Tilly." Easton motions to the dining table.

I take a seat, my eyes darting to the side when I remember what Greyson did to me in this exact spot last night.

They both pick a seat at the table, and Greyson comes up behind me, placing his hands on my shoulders, gently massaging my tense muscles.

"What's going on? Is it dad?" My heart starts to race.

Why were they being so quiet? Was something wrong?

"Tills." Adam glances at Easton.

"What?!" I screech.

Greyson squeezes my shoulder lightly. "Give him a minute, baby."

Adam locks eyes with me and my heart clenches.

"Blaine McKnight was found dead in his condo this morning."

And just when I thought it was all coming together, everything fell apart.

Chapter 41

Greyson

What. The. Fuck.

Tilly gasps, her hand flying to her mouth.

"What? What happened?"

"He didn't show up for a golf tournament, so his colleague went to check on him." Adam places his forearms on the table. "I have a buddy in Denver who was on scene. He knew you two had been together and he gave me a courtesy call."

"How did..." she hesitates. "How?"

"He was beat up pretty good, but a gunshot wound to the back of the head is what killed him." Easton briefly meets my eyes.

I drop my hands down from Tilly's shoulders, then spin round to scrub a hand down my face.

This is bad.

I was there. I hit him. My blood is probably mixed with his.

Fuck.

We fought. I won't lie about that. I threatened him. But I didn't kill him.

"Grey.." My brother's voice has me turning to face him. "If there's something you need to tell us, now is the time."

I peer down at Tilly, her eyes are filling quickly and she jumps up from the chair, crashing into my chest.

"He was sending her threatening messages last night." I let my hand cup the back of her head. "I went over to have a talk with him. It got heated. I threw a few punches, but that was it. He was alive and well when I left. I swear."

"Fuck, Greyson." Adam slams his fist on the table.

"I wasn't going to stand by and let him threaten her!" I roar. "He already put his fucking hands on her. I wish I would have been the one to kill him," I seethe.

"Can we just calm down." Easton stands. "Look, we already know the Denver PD are going to want to question you Tilly. I know y'all just split up, but I doubt anyone knows it yet."

Tilly pulls away, swiping at her face. "I haven't even seen him or spoken to him since Thursday when..." she trials off. "When he assaulted me."

Adam paces over to the living room, muttering God knows what to himself.

"Oh my God." Tilly eyes widen. "What if they think it was me? Because he hit me."

"No." I reach for her. "You had nothing to do with this. That's not even something you need to worry about."

"But you do." Adam stops pacing. "We'll do our best to keep an ear for what they find. But Grey, they might come for you. If they do you need to be ready."

Shit.

"Can y'all excuse me." Tilly slips past me, quickly jogging up the stairs.

I had to latch onto the back of the couch to keep myself in place instead of chasing after her.

"Grey." Adam's voice is steady.

"Yeah." I glance over at him.

"I'm only going to ask this once. And whatever your answer is, I'll believe it."

I knew what was coming. I face my best friend. Eye to eye.

"Did you do it?"

I hold his stare before I answer. "No."

He nods. "That's all I need to know."

My eyes move to the stairs, and he waves me off. "Take care of her. It may be a rough few days."

"Alright." I reach out to shake his hand.

He took it, then my brother approaches me. "We'll try to keep a handle on it."

"Thanks man." He gives me a hug, with a slap on the back before they both leave.

My feet carry me swiftly up the stairs, to find Tilly sitting on the floor at the foot of her bed. Tears soak her cheeks as she stares up at me. Fear slices through my heart at the expression on her face. I hate I can't control this. I take a few strides before I kneel down in front of her.

"Hey. Look at me." I cup her face.

"I'm scared." Her voice shakes.

"I won't let anything happen to you. I promise."

Her head shakes and more tears fall. "I'm not worried about me." She lands her tiny hands over mine. "Did you...." She closes her eyes. "When you went over there."

"I didn't do it. I swear to you, I didn't. I was protecting you. Yeah, I was angry...but I didn't shoot him. I don't even have a gun here."

She nods again as more tears fall. I seal my lips over hers just as my vision starts to blur. I blink, trying to clear the fuzz. I blink again as Blaine's bloody face flashes in my mind. The rest was fuzzy. The memories. I hold her to my chest, my own heaving as I sort through the events of last night.

I didn't kill Blaine McKnight, so who the fuck did?

CHAPTER 42

Tilly

After crying for almost an hour, I guess I had fallen back asleep. I didn't want to marry Blaine and I was disgusted at how he treated me, but I would never want him to die. *Murdered for God's sake.* And Greyson. He was so angry when he left. The look on his face had me worried he's do something stupid. Something out of character and a small part of me was still terrified that he lost control.

The bed was empty when I woke up. The house quiet. After forcing myself from the rumpled sheets I make my way downstairs. Greyson was on the couch, his phone to his ear. I didn't want to interrupt, so I tiptoe to the kitchen to pour myself a glass of lemonade until he hangs up.

"Hey," I say quietly.

He glances over his shoulder. "Hey. You get some rest?"

"A little."

He places his phone down on the coffee table and pushes to his feet. "That was Adam. They want you down at the station. He worked it out with his buddy that they speak with you here. Given you're Cap's daughter. They're also bringing an interpreter in case you are more comfortable signing."

I take a sip of the cold liquid. "Ok. Let me change and I'll head down there."

"I'm going with you." Greyson rounds the couch.

"I don't know if that's a good idea." He halts his steps. "I just...my fiancé was just killed in his own home, and I show up with my..." I wave a hand.

"He's your *ex-fiancé.*" His nostrils flare in frustration. "And what's happening between us is no one's business but ours."

"I know but, I'm trying to keep any heat away from you." I move towards the staircase, but he catches me by the crook of my arm.

"You're not doing this alone."

"I am. You can be pissed off all you want."

"Rosie," he warns.

"Greyson," I snap back. "I'm going in alone and that's final."

When I pull into the parking lot I hear my phone buzz. I'm sure it's a text from Greyson. He was furious I made him stay behind, but the last thing we needed was someone thinking some fatal love triangle took place and he was a scorned lover. The fact he was literally in his condo had my stomach rolling. I believed him when he said he didn't do it. What I was concerned about was what the police would perceive. I'm a cop's daughter. I'm no stranger to tactics and protocol, and just like any true crime documentary, they always suspect the spouse, fiancé, girlfriend, or significant other. It's human nature. I was ready. I had nothing to hide.

Except the fact I was letting Greyson Roy rail me into next week while my ex-fiancé was being murdered.

I stalk into the Timber Creek PD with the same attitude I would on any other day. My father was the first one to greet me. He wraps me up in a hug, then leans down to whisper in my ear.

"You ok, sweetheart?"

"I'm ok dad. A little shaken up, but I'm good," I admit.

He steps aside and motions for me to go to my brother. Adam glances behind me. I knew he was looking for Grey.

"I told him to stay." He fell in step beside me. "He wasn't happy."

"It's probably for the best right now." He places his hand on the door to an interview room. "You get uncomfortable or anything you can stop talking at any time."

"Ok." I nod.

I enter the room as two Denver detectives rise from the table.

"Ms. Harper." One points to the chair across from him. "I'm Detective Caster, this is Detective Asher." He points to the woman in the corner of the room. "This is Celine, our ASL interpreter."

I wasn't nervous until I sat down.

My stomach knots into a million tiny balls as I lift my hands. *Detectives, Celine.* I acknowledge.

"First of all, condolences on Mr. McKnight." Detective Caster folds his hands. "You two are or were recently engaged?"

We were. I sign.

"We were," Celine voices.

"Your father had mentioned your recent parting. When was the last time you saw Mr. McKnight?" He asks.

Thursday evening. I sign.

"Thursday evening," she repeats.

"Can you tell me what happened between you two?"

I lift my hands. *I have only known Blaine for about three months. It was a whirlwind. It happened fast and after I had accepted his proposal, I realized we were rushing into it.*

Celine translates to the detectives before I continue.

When I voiced my concern he got angry. He got violent, but apologized immediately. Emotions began to clog my throat as the memories were brought to the forefront of my mind. *I decided to end things with him after he pushed me into a wall. We had dinner Thursday evening. I called off the engagement and he...*

Celine passes along my words.

"Got angry?" Detective Asher asks.

Yes.

"I'm guessing he did that to your lip?" Caster offers.

I touch the spot with a frown and give a simple nod of my head.

"Where were you last night?" He asks.

I was at Officer Roy's house.

"And what time did you leave?"

About eight thirty.

Celine kept translating each time I signed.

"Can anyone corroborate what time you got home?"

I was alone.

Which was true. Technically. I walked into the house alone.

Unless one of my neighbors saw me.

Celine finishes my answer then Caster gives Asher a quick jerk of his chin.

"Do you know of anyone who would want Mr. McKnight dead?" Asher asks.

I shake my head. *No. Honestly I'm starting to believe I didn't really know him at all. I didn't go to the city often. I knew he was an attorney. I'm guessing he has made some enemies at some point.*

Asher jots down a few things on a notepad.

"Ms. Harper. Thank you for your time. If we have anymore questions, we'll reach out."

Both men stand, and I follow suit. When I reach the door, Caster speaks.

"One more thing." He pauses and his face takes on a different expression. "What is your relationship with Greyson Roy?"

Ice slithers through my veins, but I keep my composure.

We're friends. I sign casually.

"Interesting." Caster hums. "Not a friend of Mr. McKnight?"

They met recently.

Shit. Where were they going with this?

"Looks like Greyson was the last man to see him alive." His lip quirks up. "If you see him. Let him know we will want to ask him a few questions."

I swallow down the urge to vomit and sign. *I will* before I turn the knob and rush out the door.

CHAPTER 43

Greyson

Sweat drips from my forehead as I slow to a jog. I couldn't sit around while the woman I loved was being interrogated, so I went for a run to clear my head. I hadn't spent much time in the gym this last week, and even though it was off season, my training schedule stays pretty strict. I'd eased up since my first meeting with doc, but I was anxious. My thoughts and memories were all over the place. I remember him opening the door. I remember the look on his face when I flicked her ring at his chest.

"What the fuck is this?" He snarls.

"Exactly what it looks like." I growl before I snag him by the collar. "Tilly Harper doesn't exist to you anymore. Lose her number. If you even

think about speaking to her, or laying a finger on her, you're done." We were nose to nose, as I sneer my threat.

He brought his hands up in attempt to push me away. "All this for her?" He chuckles. "A deaf girl?"

I clench tighter, yanking him forward.

"Watch it," I warn.

An arrogant grin forms on his face. "She has a pretty mouth though, right?"

My vision clouds.

"My favorite is when it's wrapped around my co...."

Then it all went dark. Hectic.

When my eyes blink open, he's on his knees, blood pooling on the floor......

I come to a complete stop, my hands resting on my knees as I suck in a deep breath. I was at the edge of Tilly's driveway. I had run all the way from my mom's house. I needed to shower and change clothes and check some emails about retirement details from coach.

Her car was in the drive, so I jog up the wooden steps, entering the cabin with a new anxiety settling in.

"Rosie!" I call out.

She comes around the corner, carrying a laundry basket. She drops it, rushing over to me.

"Where'd you go?" She asks.

"I went back to the house, then went for a run." I embrace her, dropping a kiss on her head. "How'd it go? What happened?"

She steps away and picks up the laundry basket.

"Typical questions. What you would expect." She sits the basket on the table. "They know about the dinner." She grabs a pair of pants, folding them in a jumbled mess. "They asked where I was. I told them Easton's then I went home."

She pulls out another piece of clothing. Her hands shaking.

"Hey..." I wrap them in mine. "It's ok."

She tosses the shirt and looks up at me. "They asked me about you." She worries her lip. "They asked what our relationship was."

"What did you tell them?"

"That we're friends," she says quietly.

The word made my stomach turn. We were way more than fucking friends.

"You know I didn't really mean that." She reaches up to lay her hand on my chest. "I just thought that was the best way to keep it simple."

I nod in agreement. I knew she was right. "And what else?"

She takes a deep breath. "They know you were there. They said you were the last man to see him alive."

The thud in my chest pounds, like the room was closing in. Like my worst fear was unraveling before me.

"They said they wanted to ask you some questions."

I slide my hand over hers. "Alright. I can do that."

"Grey." Her eyes plead with me.

"I don't have anything to hide. I was there. I touched him. My DNA will be all over him. I can tell them what happened. The truth."

She tugs her hand from mine. "And the truth puts you in a really bad position, Greyson."

I was aware of that. Aware of how this all looks.

"It's all circumstantial," I point out.

"You need a lawyer." She attempts to look for her phone.

"No. That makes me look guilty."

She pauses and rakes her hands through her hair.

"What do we do?"

"You let me handle it." I grip her chin with my fingertips. "I just need you to trust me."

She buries her face in my chest, and I close my eyes.

Trust me. I didn't even trust myself at the moment.

CHAPTER 44

Greyson

I push open the door to the squad room. It was busy. The room buzzing as people shuffled about Timber Creek business. The first person I see is Jace, who's brows furrow when he strides towards me.

"What are you doing here?"

"I was informed they wanted to speak to me. From what I gather they know I was at Blaine's condo. I need to set the record straight on what happened." I glance around. "Is East here?"

"He's off today. But Adam is." He places his hand on my shoulder and guides me off to a side hallway.

"Greyson, I'd advise you to answer a basic yes or no. Don't give them any ammunition," he says quietly.

"It's better if I come clean than if they find out on their own right?"

"Yes, but tread carefully. I've done this a hundred times. To be honest, you'd be the first person I would look at. I asked Adam's friend; he said you were seen on surveillance cameras."

I nod, blowing out a breath.

"Just keep your cool and answer truthfully." He shrugs. "We'll try to stay in the loop. Let you know when they've cleared you."

We walk back into the squad room. Adam wanders out of Cap's office just as we step around the corner. His expression isn't comforting when he meets me halfway.

"I was just about to call you." He runs a hand over his jaw. "They want to question you."

"That's why I'm here."

Adam tilts his chin at someone across the room. Two men who didn't look like they belong in our small town.

I clench and unclench my fists as I follow Adam into an interview room. One man seems riddled with tension while the other is relaxed.

"Greyson Roy." The relaxed one sticks out his hand. "Detective Asher. I'm a big fan."

Ok not what I was expecting.

"Thanks." I shake it before facing the other man.

"I'm Detective Caster. You can have a seat," he states.

I sit down in the cold metal chair and roll my shoulders back.

"I'm sure you're aware of the news of Mr. McKnight?"

"Yes sir."

"How did you two know each other?" He asks.

"Mutual friends," I answer.

"Ms. Harper?"

"Yes."

I grit my teeth at the mention of her name. They didn't need to bring her into this. She was just as much of a victim as he was.

"I'll just cut to the chase Mr. Roy. You were the last person seen entering Mr. McKnight's condo before he was killed." He levels me with his eyes. "Why were you there?"

"I went to have a conversation."

"And did you?"

"Yes."

"What was the conversation about?" He glances at Asher.

"About his threats to Tilly. He was threatening to show back up at her house. He was already violent once and I let him know that he needed to stay away." I clear my throat.

"And how did he react to this conversation?" Asher leans back in his chair.

"As you would expect. He wasn't happy." I shrug.

My hands are resting on the table, and I don't miss Caster's eyes catch on my knuckles.

"Did you and Mr. McKnight have a physical altercation?" He asks.

"We did. I'm not going to lie to you. I landed a punch or two, then left. He was alive and well. Still spewing threats as I walked out the door."

Caster nods. "Ok. Did you happen to see anyone else? Anyone in the building that looked suspicious?"

I scrub my palms down my thighs. "No."

"Alright." He adjusts his coat. "We appreciate you coming in. It's just protocol, but we ask that you stay in town for the next few days. In case we have any more questions."

"Sure. I have no plans to go anywhere." I stand and give each one a nod before I'm back out in the squad room.

Jace and Adam come out of the adjoining room.

"You did good." Adam blows out a heavy breath and braces his hands on his hips.

"Glad that's over. Y'all need anything else? I need to get to Tilly." I fish out my phone to shoot her a text.

"That's it man. We'll let y'all know if we hear anything." He squeezes my shoulder.

I thumb out a text to her as I'm walking to the door. I almost run right into a small frantic body.

"Crap! Sorry!" I glance up to see Lucy, who apologizes quickly.

"It's my bad. I wasn't watching where I was going." I shove my phone back in my pocket.

"No worries." She gives a timid smile. "How's Tilly?" She whispers.

I figured news wouldn't stay quiet for long.

"I heard about Blaine. That's awful." She shakes her head.

"Yeah. Bad deal." I push my palm against the door. "I got to run. I'll see you later."

"Bye Grey." She waves, heading towards Rex's desk.

All I want is to get home, pull Tilly in my arms and forget about this fucking nightmare.

CHAPTER 45

Tilly

"Does he have any friends?" June presses her face up to Nelson's cage. "I have a frog he can play with."

"You don't have a frog," Elle deadpans.

"I do haves one." June presses her hands to her hips. "He's in the box under my bed."

Elle narrows her eyes. "And why was I not aware of this?"

"Daddy said it was our secret." She grins.

"Did he, now?" Elle glances over at Easton, who's talking on the phone in the corner of my living room.

Camille, Bekka, and Elle came over as soon as I got back this afternoon.

Easton had stopped by to pick up June, so the girls could spend some time with me. I think we were all shaken up at this point. Regardless of anyone's feelings towards Blaine, he still didn't deserve to be shot in the head like some vile execution.

Easton hangs up the phone and faces us with a small look of relief. "Grey just finished up. He's heading this way."

I reposition the blanket I have wrapped around me up to my neck. Camille and Bekka were knee deep in dough. They opted for chicken and dumplings for dinner and I didn't have the energy to argue. Whatever they wanted to do to pass the time was fine by me. I was exhausted and the phone call I had with Blaine's mother thirty minutes ago was heartbreaking and surprisingly typical.

I revealed the news that I had broken off the engagement before his death. She was devastated, but still managed to point out since we weren't married I would in no way receive any compensation.

Like that's what I'm concerned with. He wasn't even cold yet.

I assured her I was not concerned and then she ended with how all her plans were uprooted for the entire weekend. *Bless her heart.*

This entire situation was just plain weird. The only explanation I can come up with is someone he was involved with through work. An angry client or an unstable person he put away at one point was on the run. I wasn't sure, but one thing I was sure of, was Greyson's innocence.

Ten minutes later Greyson arrives. His hair looks like he's been running his hands through it for hours.

He doesn't speak, just hauls me close, kissing me on the lips with a gentle touch to my cheek. Dinner is quiet between the adults, but we all sit together and ate with June chatting up a storm. We needed her sweet nature to lighten the evening. She continued to use "sign language" while she spoke. She wasn't actually using correct signs, but

I joined in anyway. It warmed my heart she thought she was including me. Things may be rocky with the recent news of her biological parents, but Easton has been raising a beautiful, kind, and considerate human being. Add Elle to the mix and she's going to be one successful little girl.

After dinner was cleaned up the girls left, and only Greyson, Easton, and I remained. I curl up on the couch and Greyson drops down next to me, bringing my legs over his lap.

"So, how'd it go?" Easton asks.

"Fine. I told them the truth. Why I was there and what happened." Greyson lifts a shoulder. "I know they have a job to do. I get it. I get how things might look."

"They don't know about y'all's relationship yet." Easton places his ankle over his knee. "I know you aren't going to like what I have to say, but it's the best for the time being."

I have a hunch what he's going to say, and I can feel my body tense. Greyson's hand travels down my leg, massaging my calf.

"Might as well lay it all out," he suggests.

Easton's eyes meet mine, then move to Grey's. "You two are going to have to cool it for a while."

"Not happening," Greyson grumbles, his hand clenching my calf.

"Brother, I'm trying to help you," Easton argues.

"I understand that, but what if whoever did this to Blaine wants to hurt Tilly?"

"Grey." I reach for his hand.

The last thing I want is to spend time apart, but I know Easton is right. At the moment, we look sketchy as hell, and I wouldn't allow anything to fall on Greyson.

"He's right." I was so close I could almost count the gold flecks in his eyes. "I know it's not ideal, but…"

"Ideal," he scoffs, standing up from the couch.

I give East a soft apology as I stand, and Greyson storms up the stairs.

"Just let me talk to him." I toss down the blanket that I was curled up with.

"I'm sorry this is happening, Tills. Sooner they find who did this, the better." He gives me a sympathetic look before grabbing his coat and leaving out the front door.

With a heavy sigh I ascended the stairs. Greyson Roy was about to be very unhappy with me.

CHAPTER 46

Tilly

When I make it to my room, Greyson is staring out my bedroom window. His broad back is to me, and I can see the tension coiling between his shoulder blades. I kick off my shoes, crossing the wood floor in my fuzzy socks decorated with cherries.

My arms wrap around his waist, and I place a kiss on his spine over his shirt.

Pressing my forehead to his back, I whisper. "Talk to me."

"I don't want to be away from you." He pauses. "I've already wasted so much time. Been gone way too long and we finally have a fucking chance...." I feel him tense, and his hand slides up over my forearm.

"It's not forever," I reassure him.

He turns to face me.

"It's just until this whole thing is sorted out and neither of us are in the spotlight."

I take in his lightly dusted jaw and the thick black lashes that line his eyes. He's incredibly beautiful. Perfect lips. Perfect straight nose. *Perfect hands.* The ones that are currently tracing the dip in my collarbone.

"I want to sleep next to you," he murmurs as he watches the movement of his fingers. "I want to wake up next to you." His fingers travel up my neck, then grasp at the scrunchy that's tied in my hair.

Heat floods my entire body as our chests meet. My scrunchy is tossed to the side and both of his hands are now in my hair.

"If I'm going to have to endure the pure torture of being away from you, at least let me have a taste to hold me over." He places a soft kiss on my lips, the pleading of more when his tongue coaxes against mine.

My nipples harden, scrapping against his chest as he lightly tugs my head back, causing my neck to be exposed.

He leans down, running his nose along my skin, then back up until he reaches my ear.

Soft nips make me shiver, and I reach out, palming his hard cock over his jeans. I stroke a few times before he lets out a low growl in my ear.

"Is that what you want?" He rasps.

"Yes." My hands move, flicking open the button with ease.

He allows me to wrench them down his thighs, and his fist automatically wraps around his shaft.

"I want to see you, Rosie." His breath is heavy as he strokes himself.

I discard my clothes in a matter of seconds, and again, I'm standing bare in front of the only man to ever make me feel this way. This *hot.* This out of breath and he hasn't even touched me. He reaches for me, moving me to the side with his free hand before he's laying back on the bed.

Still stoking himself he smirks. "Get that sweet ass over here and sit on my face."

My cheeks flush and I gasp. I've *never* done that before.

"Grey...I don't think that's very safe." My brows furrow.

I'll suffocate him. Then that's another man dead who was involved with me. I'd be incarcerated by morning.

"Why is it not safe?" He questions, still grinning at me like the cat who caught the canary.

"Don't you like.... need to breathe?"

He chuckles. "I though you trusted me."

I shift on my feet. "I do. But..."

"But nothing." He let's go of his cock and reaches out to grab me by my hips. "Sit. On. My. Face."

Before I can react, I'm hoisted in the air, then I'm straddling his head. My hands instinctively grip onto the headboard, and he kisses my thigh.

"Alright baby. Let's see how loud you can scream."

As soon as his tongue meets my throbbing center, I'm electrified. My body screams as I start to move my hips, chasing the release I know I desperately need. My nerves are shot, my muscles tight, and right now all I want is to feel that overwhelming bliss.

I rock my hips, and he hums his approval, flicking the spot that makes my thighs quiver.

My muscles clench as my climax rises to the surface. My moans get louder, my fingernails dig into the wooden bed frame all while his tongue unravels every single ounce of anxiety I have.

My hair hangs down my back, tickling the skin above my tailbone as I tilt my head back, letting the moment flow over me. The moment right before I know I'm about to come all over Greyson Roy's face.

Then it hits. Pure euphoria as a scream lurches from my throat. His arms brace down over my thighs as my body shakes, and after what feels like a million unhinged seconds later, I fall limp against the headboard.

I'm breathing hard, my face is smushed against the wood, and I'm so dazed I haven't even given a thought to if Greyson is alive underneath me. I abruptly sit up as I swipe the damp hair from my face. I feel his arms tighten on my legs and when I look down to meet his eyes his lips are shining with my release. He smiles again, then runs his tongue over his bottom lip before commanding. "Again."

CHAPTER 47

Greyson

Tilly slumps over, her heart pounding as she gasps. "I can't, Grey."

She just gifted me with her third orgasm, and I finally give her a little mercy. I let her climb off of me, but not before I'm hovering over her satisfied body.

"I think you can, Rosie." I run my palm over her smooth skin. "One more."

She groans, but her body betrays her because she opens those long legs, allowing me to slide inside of her in one smooth thrust.

She cries out, her hands grasping at my back. My lips meet hers, kissing and nipping as I slide in and out of the last woman I plan on *ever* having this part of me.

Somewhere between her roaming hands and our tongues dancing, my hips slow. I'm no longer thrusting as wildly as I can, I'm slowly burying myself to the hilt, just to slowly pull back out. I don't think

I've ever *made love* before, but fuck, if this is it, I'll make love to her every day for the rest my life. I pull away from her lips, letting my gaze get lost in her blue eyes. I don't have to ask if we'll get through this. I don't have to ask if she'll still be mine. *I can feel it.*

"I love you," I whisper, pressing my hips against hers.

She whimpers before breathing out, "I love you, too."

Then it's skin, sweat, rapid heartbeats, and groans of pleasure as she gives me what I asked for.

One more.

I spend two hours wrapped around her. Trying to pour out seven years worth of feelings in the small window of time. I waited until her breathing grew even and she was fast asleep. Then I got dressed and went home.

Alone.

When I walk in, my mother is sitting on the couch in some kind of mint green paste that looks like dried mud. She's dressed in a white robe with a full glass of wine perched in her hand. *Fried Green Toma-toes*, a movie she's watched at least a thousand times over my life span is playing on the TV. I would never admit it to the general public, but it's a damn good movie.

"Greyson! Sit." She pats the couch cushion next to her.

Mom was always the softer parent. The one who gave me nothing but encouragement. Never criticism. No matter how bad of a game I played.

"You look tired, son." She smiles, causing the goop on her face to crack.

"I *am* tired, mom." I sigh and plop down beside her.

"Me too." She taps my leg and I turn to face her.

It hasn't been that long since she kicked my father out. I knew she was still grieving a thirty year marriage that was flushed down the drain.

"I'm so sorry for what he did to you," I tell her honestly. "I've been really angry at him."

The day he barged into my meeting at the end of the season, acting like his job was to ensure I got the best. Bullshit. He wanted control, just like always. Control of my contract, my agents, my endorsements. For the first time in my life, I didn't let him have it, and it turned ugly, fast.

"I'll be ok, Grey. I got you boys, my June bug, and Ellie. My friends, a roof over my head and a hefty pile in the bank because my lawyer knew her stuff."

She chuckles lightly. "I need to send Whitley a thank you basket for recommending her. She's pretty savvy on divorces."

Whitley works for a DA's office in California and even though she didn't have the label, she was just as sharp and cutthroat.

"I'm sure she'd love that." I push to my feet. "I'm going to crash. You free tomorrow for lunch?"

"Sure. I'm assuming we need to discuss why you were being questioned at the police station."

I run a hand through my hair. "Yeah, and a few other things that have recently unfolded."

Like I'm retiring and plan on marrying Tilly Harper as soon as physically possible.

"Night, Grey."

"Night, mom."

I trudge up the stairs and fall into bed.

I didn't sleep a damn wink.

Chapter 48

Tilly

It had been four days. I'd went months without seeing Greyson. Went years without speaking verbal words to him, but just after four days of only seeing him through the office window once when he had his volunteer day, I feel like I've been hit by a truck. *I ached.* My heart *ached.* And I hated that we had to do this. We sucked at timing. Always had. I guess I shouldn't have expected anything less.

My day is almost over, and I'm exhausted. Blaine's mom had been updating me with funeral arrangements and I felt like a terrible human being because I had zero desire to go.

I shut off my computer and grab my phone when I hear a familiar voice. I pause, thinking I was absolutely losing it when my suspicions were made correct.

"I can't believe Frank still refuses to install lights in the parking lot. I've told him countless times it's a lawsuit waiting to happen."

Whitley casually walks through the door, looking just as professional as she did the courtroom.

Maroon pantsuit, paired with heeled boots and painted lips. The definition of *head bitch in charge.*

Whit. I sign because tears are clogging my throat as I rush around my desk and launch myself at her.

"I thought you had a no tears rule?" She muses.

I let out a sob that turns into laughter because, God, I miss her so much.

"All I've done is cry for the last two weeks," I mumble as I wipe my eyes with the sleeve of my shirt. "I hate crying."

"I know. You get that from me." She pushes her brown hair over her shoulder. "You ready?"

"What are you even doing here?" I pick up my purse and shove my phone inside.

"Dad called." She gives me a knowing look. "I hear it's a real shit show."

"Yeah, that's one way to put it." I flip off the light.

"Good thing he's making your favorite tonight."

"Dinner?"

"Yes. Everyone is coming." She smiles.

Everyone. Everyone but him.

The house is already filled with chatter and laughter when we enter. The aroma of a home cooked meal fills the house as I follow Whitley into the foyer. Camille sits at the bar next to Jace, and Adam is digging around in the fridge. Bekka is at the kitchen table with Elle and Nayna, I'm sure getting an earful of advice they didn't ask for. My grandmother had just returned from a two week long "retreat". She's a sex/relationship therapist so I haven't even had the nerve to ask her how it went. I'm sure she will share entirely too much information and I'll be scarred for life.

I scan my eyes to the other side of the room to see Easton is in deep conversation with my father.

The warmth from every smile and conversation washes over me, but I still feel cold. Something is missing. As soon as the thought crosses my mind, I feel an arm snake around my waist. His cologne fills the air in the entry way, and I'm tugged backwards, then pressed up against the wall. Greyson's golden eyes collide with mine, showing every ounce of misery I've been feeling the last four days. I don't speak.

Just lift my hands. *Hey.*

His eyes remain on mine as he lifts his. *Hey, baby.*

His forehead drops, resting against mine.

"I've missed you so much," he whispers.

I move my hands again because I know if I speak, I'll cry, and I was determined not to cry anymore.

I missed you t......

Before I even finished his lips are on mine. His kiss is soft, yet possessive. Filled with promises that I cling to like it's the actual air I need to breathe.

He slides his hands up my back, cupping my head with one hand as the kiss slowly comes to an end.

"I hate this, you know. I fucking hate it," he mutters.

I know. Me too. I sign before I intertwine our fingers.

He raises our hands to his lips, marking a quick kiss on my knuckles as we make our way towards the rowdy group.

But just when I thought we'd have one regular night with friends and family, a knock sounds at the door.

Greyson whirls on his heels to answer while I stop at the entrance to the living room. My breath hitches when he opens the door and I see who stands behind it. Detective Caster and Detective Asher meet him with a curious stare.

"Greyson Roy. Just the man we were looking for."

CHAPTER 49

Greyson

I find myself seated on the same steel chair from four days ago, except this time the tension in the air is suffocating. The way these two detectives eye me while flipping through a red folder makes me shift in my seat. I agreed to come. Agreed to answer any more questions they had, but I've been sitting here watching them in silence for a solid fifteen minutes. *I'm starting to get frustrated.*

"You admitted to going to Mr. McKnight's residence. Is that correct?" Detective Caster flips another page.

"That's correct." I nod.

"And you stated he was alive when you left?"

"That's correct."

He places the folder on the table. "Is that the first time you and Mr. McKnight had an altercation?"

I furrow my brows. "Yes."

"You sure?" He questions.

"Yes."

"Interesting." He crosses his arms. "We have a witness claiming they saw you and Mr. McKnight last week outside The Peak. It looked heated and you grabbed him."

The family dinner.

I don't remember anyone even being on the street that night, nor in the alley.

"We had words. There were no punches thrown," I offer.

"And what were those words about?" His arms uncross. "Ms. Harper?"

I don't like his tone, or his arrogance that suddenly appears.

"Yes."

"You seem awfully protective of her." He leans his elbows down on the table and jerks his chin up with a smirk. "You fucking her?"

I can't control the slam of my fist on this rickety table before I point my finger at him. "Watch it."

He holds his palms up. "Just a question."

This time it's Detective Asher that goes for the jugular. "We have a theory, Greyson."

I relax back in the chair, acting as natural as I can.

"We think you and Ms. Harper were having an affair. Blaine found out. He obviously got violent with her in which you retaliated. You went to his condo, there was a physical assault before pressing a gun to the back of his head and you pulled the trigger."

"We know you're in love with Ms. Harper. He hurt her. You got angry." Caster interjects. "Seems you have some anger issues. The recent altercation with your father? Now this?"

"You tossed the gun in the dumpster on your way out, and now your problem was solved. Blaine got what he deserved, now you and Ms. Harper could live happily ever after," Asher finishes.

I nod a few times, entertaining their bogus theory. "One problem, detectives." I clash eyes with Caster. "I don't have a gun here. Any weapon I own is locked in my safe in San Antonio."

Asher reaches down, presenting a plastic evidence bag, then slides it on the table between us. Inside is a black pistol.

"You may not, but Ms. Harper does, and your DNA is all over it."

What?

There was a knock at the door, and they both stand, taking the gun with them before leaving me alone again. Something wasn't adding up, and this was turning out to be way more serious than I thought.

I sit with my head in my hands. My elbows planted on the cold tabletop. I never expected to be in this room. Never expected for things to turn out the way they did. The grinding sound of the thirty year old hinges has me lifting my head. My heavy eyes snag on the pair of shoes that enter the room. I let out a solid breath before I lean back in my chair.

Slowly, I meet the eyes of my brother. A man I would trust with my life. He braces his palms on the table across from me, head bowed, and shoulders bunched. Tension rolls off of him in waves, wrapping tight around my throat.

"It's not looking good, Grey." His hoarse voice meets my ears and I clam up. Sweat breaks out on the back of my neck and my stomach rolls with nausea.

"The evidence is stacked against you." He lifts his head. "What the fuck happened?"

I shake my head, running a hand over my face. "It's not what it looks like, East."

He stands tall, his hands hanging by his side. "I can only do so much. It's too close to home. The sheriff will step in. Then it's out of our hands."

I nod. "I understand."

"I don't think you do, brother." He pauses. "They're going to charge you."

I clench my fists. "I was protecting her."

Just like I promised.

"It doesn't matter. What matters is what they can prove." His eyes penetrate me with a pity I hate. "And right now, the evidence proves it was you."

The door swings open yet again and a man I've never seen struts through the door. He's wearing a business suit, an expensive one. He approaches the table, dropping a leather brief case down as he adjusts his cuff links.

"Don't say another word to them." He glances at Easton who glances at me.

"I'm sorry, who are you?" I ask.

He holds out his hand. "Jordan Carmichael. Your attorney."

"I didn't hire an attorney," I counter.

"I did." A voice comes from the door.

Jace stands in the frame. He and Jordan share a look before he speaks again. "He's my brother."

CHAPTER 50

Tilly

"This is ridiculous. I'm going down there." My purse is on my shoulder and I'm storming towards the hall before anyone else can contest.

The anyone being Camille and Whitley. After the detectives showed up, I couldn't even eat. Which in turn made me feel guilty dad had put all the work into making my favorite meal. He, Easton, Jace, and Adam left right after Greyson did. They went to the station to find out what's going on. I've been a giant ball of anxiety for the last hour and a half, and I can't handle it anymore.

"We're coming too." Whitley and Camille follow with the same amount of concern woven into their expressions.

A quick ten minute drive and we're out of the car and entering the squad room. I immediately feel the hostility. Adam looks furious as he talks on the phone at his desk and Rex is trying to appease the two detectives from Denver.

I take a few steps towards my father's office when Easton, Greyson, and a man I don't know step out from an interview room.

His eyes meet mine and I move to go to him, but Camille catches me by the arm.

"You're still being questioned Mr. Roy."

Caster makes his way across the room, but the man in a suit steps in front of Greyson with all the arrogance of the entire NFL football teams combined.

"He's cooperated and answered your questions. You can either charge him, or my client is free to go." He switches the briefcase to his other hand. "From what I can tell everything you have is circumstantial."

Asher pulls out his phone, holding it up to his ear as Caster and the man I'm assuming is Greyson's attorney, banter back and forth.

"What are the fucking odds?" Whitley scoffs behind me, but I'm too caught up on what's transpiring in front of me.

My father steps out of his office. Adam has now joined the commotion and all I want to do is run into Greyson's arms. To make this all go away.

"Arrest him." Asher hangs up the phone.

Caster pulls out a pair of cuffs and I can feel every nerve in my body pinch. Pain and agony rushing straight through my bones.

"Greyson Roy. You are under arrest for the murder of Blaine McKnight. Anything you say can and will be used against you in a court of law."

The tears burst like a dam, and I sob out. My feet bring me closer, and my hands fly up. *He didn't do it. He was with me.*

"Tilly!" My brother calls as I push through two officers.

Caster is almost to Greyson when he lifts his hands to me. *Stop, Rosie.*

I ignore him, my tears flowing faster just as my father steps in my path.

"Tilly, Sweetheart, calm down." His hands grip my shoulders, but I fight against him. Pushing and shoving anything that's keeping me from Greyson.

Dad, stop this please! I beg with my hands.

He shakes his head and I stretch my neck to see around him. Greyson places his hands behind his back, his chin held high and his eyes hard. He doesn't fight it. He lets Caster place the silver cuffs on his wrists and another sob wretches from my throat.

This can't be real. This *can't* be happening. Not now. Not when we just began.

His eyes meet mine briefly. He gives no emotion away, but my hands lift on their own. *I love you.*

My dad wraps his arms around me, tugging me into his chest as they walk Greyson out the door. I let out my frustration, my pain, my anger, all into the man who's loved me unconditionally from day one. I feel his hands on my cheeks, and he lifts my face.

"It's not over, Tilly. We're going to fight. I need you to be strong. Can you do that?"

I nod absently.

I can.

I can for him.

CHAPTER 51

Tilly

I pull myself together. By a thread. Swipe my face and give my attention to the attorney who is standing face to face with my sister who looks absolutely feral.

"What the hell are you doing here?" Whitley's hands shoot to her hips.

"Doing my job," he deadpans. "I could ask you the same thing."

"This is my hometown. Tilly is my sister." She motions. "How do you know Greyson?"

"I don't." He checks his gold watch like he's over the conversation already.

"What do you mean you don't?" She questions. "You flew all the way from California for a man you don't even know?"

"Are you done playing twenty questions? Is this how Sutton runs his office? No wonder he's always behind."

Whitley throws her hands up and faces me. "Who hired him?"

"I did." Jace rests on a desk, a smirk across his face at the unexpected showdown taking place.

"Well, a little insight on Mr. Carmichael here." Whitley hikes a thumb over her shoulder. "He's an arrogant prick who has no respect for the law. He plays by his own rules and doesn't give a shit who he crushes in the process."

"In other words. I'm good," he supplies.

"Good? You mean manipulative? Underhanded?" Whitley faces him. "Should I go on?"

"I think that's enough, cupcake. You're making me blush." He winks.

Jace barks out a laugh and then the only man I've ever seen to render Whitley Harper speechless walks to me. "I'm Jordan Carmichael." He shifts his eyes to Whitley. "Jace's brother."

The shocked gasp from Whitley's mouth echos across the room.

"Different dads." He answers the question before anyone can ask why their last names are different.

"You mind if we sit down and talk?" He asks me.

I nod, signing *yes*, because he makes me nervous.

I can tell he doesn't understand, so Camille steps in. "I can help translate." She holds out her hand. "I'm Camille."

"I know. Hats off to you for handling this one." He tips his chin towards Jace before he looks back to me. "After you."

After a lengthy conversation, midway through my nerves calmed enough for me to be able to speak verbally to Jordan without wanting to crawl in a hole and never come out. This was important for Greyson, so I decided it was time I set my insecurities aside. For the moment at least. I needed to be strong. To be straight forward and voice the truth.

"The only thing solid right now is the murder weapon." Jordan looks up at me. "How did your gun get into Blaine's condo?"

"I have no idea." I ran through the last week in my mind. "The last time I saw it was the night Blaine came to dinner and I called things off." I close my eyes. "I had pulled it out of my drawer and told him to leave. He had already hit me and was dragging me by my hair when I elbowed him in the ribs."

I pop open my eyes. "Greyson showed up. He helped me get upstairs and into the shower then he cleaned up." My eyes dart to his. "Everything was clean when I got back downstairs, and the gun was no longer on the floor."

"So, he picked it up?" Camille asks.

"He must have. That's why his fingerprints are on it. He must have put it back where I keep it."

"Ok. Did you check the drawer again?" Jordan asks.

"No." I sigh defeated.

"It's ok. I'm just trying to see every possibility." He scrubs a hand over his stubble. "Who else knows you have a gun and where it is?"

"Just my family. Cami, Adam, Dad. Whit may, I'm not sure." I shrug.

Different scenarios race through my brain then I freeze. It never even occurred to me.

"The blackouts," I mumble.

"The what?" Cami rubs her hand across my back, trying to soothe me.

"He's been...." I pause not knowing how much I should share. It's private, but this seems like something Jordan should know.

"His injuries?" Jordan asks.

I nod.

"He told me. I needed to know everything, and he admitted to having symptoms lately. That may help us or hurt us. Depends on which way the prosecutor wants to go."

Dread pulls at my heart. For the first time I'm actually sitting here considering it.

That Greyson may have actually killed my ex-fiancé.

Chapter 52

Greyson

I spent my first night in jail. It was a picnic compared to the gut wrenching tears I watched roll down Tilly's face as she witnessed me get cuffed. I hated she saw me like that. *Like I was some monster.* And maybe I was. The more I tried to retrace my steps, the more unsure I became. I knew my confusion and lost time had happened once or twice. Could it have happened that night? Was I so angry that it clouded my judgement? My control? Did I take that gun?

The arraignment went just as Jordan suspected. Because of my status, and wealth, they decided I was a risk. Bail was denied and I was hauled back to this steel box until I stand trial or Jordan could get the charges dismissed. He seems like a man who knows his shit. I trust Jace, so in turn, my trust is in him to do whatever he's got to do.

"Roy. You got a visitor." The guard opens my cell, so I unfold myself from the hard as fuck bed and follow him through the hall.

He leads me to a room that's lined with chairs on one side. On the other side of the glass is more chairs.

"Fourth one down," he directs.

I walk, my hands still in cuffs as I approach the chair. When I sit down, a door opens on the other side and Tilly steps through.

Her eyes look swollen from crying. She tries to hide them under her Timber Creek PD hat, but I still see it. The exhaustion. The emotional turmoil. All because of me.

She sits down, and instead of grabbing the phone attached to the wall, she lifts her hands.

I'm so sorry, Grey. Are you ok?

I couldn't move my hands well, but I did the best I could.

You have nothing to be sorry for.

She yanks on the hoodie she's wearing. *My hoodie.* Before she signs again.

We're going to get you out of here. I promise.

What if I deserve it? I ask.

You don't. You were protecting me.

I drop my head. She looks so broken. So scared. What if I was convicted? What if I spent the rest of my life in a jail cell?

She didn't deserve weekly visits on the other side of a fucking glass window. She deserved so much more, and I thought it was the right time. A time when I could actually give it to her.

A loud thud sounds against the glass. I lift my head to see her raised from the chair.

Look at me. She waves her hand over her face. *Do not give up on me.*

What if I'm in here? What if I'm the monster they're saying I am? I ask.

Her hands shake. She's growing angrier by the second and I was sinking further away. Into that dark part of my mind.

Don't wait for me, Rosie.

It killed me. I wasn't even saying the words aloud, but it split me in two.

If this goes south, you don't need to waste your time on me. You keep living.

Multiple tears slide down her cheeks as she slams her hand against the glass again.

No! You don't get to decide for me anymore!

My throat clogs. This whole thing was too much. Too many regrets. Not enough time.

I love you. I sign. *No matter what happens, I love you.*

I feel the dampness on my cheeks. I can't even remember the last time I actually cried, but I can't hold them back. Here I was in an orange jumpsuit, charged with murder, while the woman I had loved for almost a decade stood on the other side. Just out of reach. Like she's always been.

I swipe at my face with the back of my hand, and she leans down, close enough I could count every wet eyelash lining her ocean eyes.

She's so calm. Staring at me hard enough I almost can't bear it.

Then she lifts those dainty hands. *I will never apologize for doing what's best for you.*

Then she turns and walks away. Leaving me so damn proud and broken all at the same time.

CHAPTER 53

Tilly

I couldn't sleep. I spent all night googling and researching before I passed out. I think I slept for about two hours when the morning sun peeked through my curtains.

My fingers rub at my heavy eyes before I blink, staring at the ceiling. My eyes trace over the woodwork. The cedar that was smoothed and carved to make this beautiful home. I scan, passing the air vent. Something catches my eye, and I jerk my gaze back, squinting hard at the bronze colored cover.

Something urges me to get up, so I do. I run downstairs to grab a screwdriver, before jogging back to drag my desk chair across the room. I slowly climb, then use the tool to unscrew the vent. Something had reflected for a split second when I scanned over it earlier and that voice in my head wouldn't shut up.

The last screw is tight, but I keep twisting until it finally let loose. My fingers grip the metal, working it away from the ceiling so I can get a clear view inside.

My stomach sours immediately. I'm face to face with a small black object. *A small camera.* I have to swallow down the urge to puke as I pluck the device out. It's wireless and the small lens must have been what hit the light just right.

My brows furrow and then the realization occurs. *I've been watched. Seen. Violated.* Private moments.

I cover my mouth, jumping down from the chair as I rush to the bathroom. I heave up what little food I have in my system. *Blaine.* How could he have done this? Watching me? I knew he was getting controlling, but this? This is crossing the line. This is intrusive. This is *wrong*.

I knew what I had to do. I pick myself up off the floor, got dressed, and then headed down to the station. Something wasn't adding up.

I storm into the squad room, not even bothering to wave at Myra, the receptionist. Rex's eyes widen when he sees me, and I stop in the middle of the room.

"Can someone tell me where my brother is?" I ask.

The entire room falls silent. I had never spoken this loudly and this public......ever.

Rex let a small smile hit his lips. "He's back here. Come on."

I quickly stay on his heels, and he leads me to a room where my brother and Easton, along with Jace and Jordan have documents and pictures scattered everywhere.

I dig out the plastic bag in my purse. "I found this hidden camera in my bedroom this morning."

Adam leans up. "You found what?"

I hand him the bag. "Blaine was watching me. Videoing me without my knowledge."

"What the fuck?" Easton scoffs.

"I don't know if there's more, but I want them gone and I want to know where the footage is being sent and stored." I drop my bag. "What's all this?" I point to the papers.

"I got my buddy to send over what they had for Jordan. We've had a small break. There was lipstick found on the collar of Blaine's shirt. They're running DNA now."

"Oh, so he was a cheater too?" I hiss under my breath.

"I know that's hard to hear, but his neighbor across the hall was out of town the last few days. She just got back. She told officers she saw a woman entering his apartment late Thursday night."

I rub my hands together. "Ok, this is good right? Is she being looked at?"

"I mean, they already charged Grey. Unless we have solid proof that it wasn't him, we're still in the same boat. There was no other DNA on the murder weapon."

"We've also looked at the medical angle. He's been to the doctor. Had symptoms. If we have to, we can use that as a defense." Jordan supplies.

"That means he's admitting he did it? That he's guilty?" I ask hoarsely.

"My job Tilly, is to prove reasonable doubt." He motions to the papers. "That's what we're working on. That camera can help."

I nod.

"The autopsy hasn't been concluded yet or they haven't released the information, but I should have a time of death soon." Adam adds. He reaches up and squeezes my shoulder. "Let me get this to IT."

I shrug off my coat and face the three men in the room. "Let's get to work."

CHAPTER 54

Greyson

I'm lying on a mattress that's as thin as my patience when my cell clangs open.

"Get up, Roy." The guard commands.

I have no clue what time it is. There are no windows where I'm at, so I stand and hold out my wrists.

He shakes his head. "No need. You're being released."

"Released?" I repeat.

"Yep. Charges were dropped." He smacks his gum. "Let's roll, got shit to do today."

I don't argue, I follow him out and down the hall as whistles and yells sound behind me. No one gives me any information as I'm given my clothes, my phone, and everything I came in here with. With a quick dismissal like I wasn't labeled a cold blooded murderer as of three minutes ago, I'm let out into a parking lot, with the sun barely rising above the sky.

I glance around and Adam comes striding up from his truck.

"Grey." He nods, embracing me when he gets to me. He slaps my back, then pulls away.

"What the hell is going on? I've been released?"

He pulls out his phone and starts to the truck.

"There's been some major developments in the last twenty-four hours, but we gotta get back to Timber Creek."

We hop in his Ford, and he's in reverse before I even get the door closed. My shoes aren't even tied, so I reach down, tying the strings as we leave the gates.

"Start from the top," I grumble.

"First thing, and do not freak the fuck out," he says, which now has my muscles bunched and I'm ready to do just that when he gets out these next words.

"Someone put hidden cameras in Tilly's house."

I clench my fists. "Fucking cameras?" I roar. "I swear, if he wasn't already dead."

"That's the thing Grey. It wasn't Blaine." He slows down, flipping on his blinker.

"What do you mean it wasn't him?" I turn in my seat.

"Those cameras lead back to an address in Mountain Lake."

"Mountain Lake? That's two towns away? Who does she know in Mountain Lake?"

"The cameras were meant to watch Tilly, but they also caught something that saved your ass." He glances at me. "They rushed the autopsy. Him being as well known as he was helped. Time of death was estimated to be around two AM."

"Ok." I try to process the information.

"You entered through the front of Blaine's condo, but you never left out of the front," he points out.

"I went out back. The front was closed off for maintenance." I remember the yellow signs and the taped off area.

"Right. But there was a camera hidden in Tilly's living room. It places you back at the house by twelve forty-five AM."

I rub my hand across my jaw at the memory of what I was doing at that exact time. I had Tilly spread out on the dining room table.

I clear my throat. "I uh.... Did you watch the video?"

He shoots me a look. "When I realized my best friend was about to fuck my sister? No. We skipped past that part."

"I appreciate that." I blow out a breath.

"That's not all." We're on the main road now, running about seventy. "It's what was caught when we were all at Easton's."

His tone makes me tense. "Someone came into the house. Deactivated the alarm, walked straight over to the drawer, and took the gun."

"The fuck?"

"Grey...." He jerks the wheel, passing a minivan. "It was a woman."

My head spins. My heart pounds.

"A woman?"

"Yeah. The same woman that was seen at his condo after you left." He swallows. "She left lipstick on his collar. DNA should be back any minute."

"None of this makes sense?" I face the window. "What woman would want Blaine dead? And why would they use Tilly's gun to do it?"

"Mistress maybe?" Adam shrugs. "I don't know I just feel like there's something we're missing."

A shrill alert sounds on my phone, and I dig it out of my pocket. My entire body goes rigid when I see the alert.

Fire.

The alerts to Tilly's security system are connected to my phone. It only alerts on an emergency. All I can do is angle the phone his way before I'm banging my fist on the dash.

"Hold on, Grey." Adam presses on the gas. "Call Easton."

CHAPTER 55

Tilly

I spent as long as I could examining every avenue possible before Adam sent me home. I took a hot bath, lit a few calming candles downstairs and drifted to sleep on the couch. I woke up in the early hours of the morning and climbed upstairs and passed out again.

I was in a deep sleep, but something was gnawing at me to wake up. I blink open my eyes, trying to let them adjust to the dark room. I roll over, glancing at the foot of my bed. My heart slams against my chest as I lurch up, taking in the dark silhouette standing at the edge. My hands move quick to flip on my lamp, hoping it's just sleep deprivation and I was hallucinating. Blaine was gone. He couldn't hurt me anymore.

I sigh in relief and my hand lands on my chest.

I snatch up my hearing aids and plug them in. "Jesus Lucy. You scared the crap out of me. Is everything ok?"

She doesn't move at first. She just stares at me with a blank expression on her face.

"Lucy? Is something wrong at the center?" I ask and fling off the comforter.

I notice a small sliver of light shining through the curtains, so I know it's morning. She should be at the office by now.

When I stand to my feet, I notice something in her hand. The lamp light reflects of the silver blade she has resting at her side. The relief I felt dissolves and fear takes its place. Swallowing me whole.

"Lucy?"

"Everything isn't okay, Tilly." Her voice is quiet, but the look in her eyes is off.

"What do you mean?" I take a small step, keeping my voice calm.

"After all I've done for you." She lets out an erratic laugh.

She's barefoot, wearing dark pants, and a dark sweatshirt. Her hair is matted, and her mascara is smeared.

"You do a lot for me, Lucy. I'm always grateful." I casually glance to see where my phone is. It's on my nightstand, but not close enough I can grab it without her noticing.

She lifts the hand that holds the knife, scratching her temple. "I did you a favor. I saved you."

What the hell is she talking about?

Her voice raises. "Blaine was garbage. He was an abusive asshole who didn't deserve to breathe the same air as you."

I open my mouth to speak, but she keeps going. Her eyes grow wilder by the second. "I saved you from him. Gave him what he deserved, and the second I do you let that rich boy that left you high and dry take his turn." She laughs again, tugging at her hair.

"Lucy, I don't understand...." I start.

"You don't understand!" She shouts.

I flinch as she stalks towards me, rushing me until I'm backed against my dresser. "They were both worthless. They both hurt you and you just let them back in after *I'm* the one who took care of you!" She taps her chest with the tip of the blade. "I'm the one who always made sure you had everything you needed. I made sure you weren't stressed at work. I made sure you had your favorite flowers every week." Her eyes seared into mine.

Angry and out of control.

The flowers?

"The flowers were from Blaine." I grip the dresser, mentally trying to picture what objects are behind me that I can grab if she decides to use that knife.

"Ha!" She reaches up and moves a piece of my hair with the sharp point. "You think that self centered bastard took time out of his day to send you flowers?" She shakes her head. "That was *me.*"

What the hell is happening?

"I really appreciate that, Lucy. I had no idea they were from you." I try flattery. Maybe she'll relax.

"They were. Because *I* love you." Her eyes start to water.

"I love you too, Luce. We're friends." I try to smile through the tremors wracking my body.

She pulls at her hair again. "I don't want to be your friend!" She shouts. "You were so kind to me. When I met you. No one took time for me. Put aside hours a day to be with me. But you did."

"Lucy, I was your teacher. That was my job."

"No!" She growls. "Then you made sure I could work with you. You wanted me there, Tilly. You needed me."

I try to slip around her, but she shoves me back, pointing the knife at my chest. "I had it all taken care of. Blaine was gone, that football player in jail. We could finally be together."

This woman is downright mental.

She thinks she loves me.

Shit.

"But you just had to go and ruin it." She sneers. "Finding those cameras that I put in place to keep you safe." Her expression changes and her eyes darken. "I watched you two. Right over there." She points to the bed. "What you let him do to you. I was sick." Her lip rises into a snarl. "He doesn't deserve you."

My eyes widen. "Why? Why would you do this?"

She steps closer. "Because I love you." She says it like it's the most truthful thing in the world. "I killed for you. And you love me." Her eyes narrow. "We were meant to be together."

I've never once had an inkling Lucy wasn't stable.

She was always so *normal.* A good friend even.

Her hand reaches up to touch my cheek. The knife tip is now digging into the cotton of my shirt. I can feel the tip about to break skin.

"Lucy," I whisper. "Please put down the knife."

I swallow down the lump of fear in my throat as she leans in closer. "I'm here now. Come away with me."

I let her chest fall flush with mine, then when I feel her relax a half a second, I take all the strength I have, lifting my forearms to slam them against her shoulders. The knife slices into me, the pain causing me to cry out, but she stumbles back, and I use the opportunity to sprint for the open door.

She screams my name, but I'm already onto the landing. I can feel the blood oozing down my chest, but I make it to the stairs, jogging down as quickly as I can. I hit the bottom, going straight for my drawer. I open it, reaching inside for my gun.

Damn it.

I forgot it was the murder weapon used to kill Blaine. That *Lucy* used to kill Blaine. Panicked, I start for the kitchen, but my foot snags on the rug in the hall. I trip, stumbling to the ground before I'm pushing back to my feet. I get one step onto the hardwood when I'm tackled from behind. Lucy lands on my back, arms around my stomach.

"Lucy!" I shriek. "Stop!"

She squeezes, but I manage to use my elbow to bust her nose. She groans, loosening her hold just enough for me to wiggle up a few inches. I turn my head to the side to catch my breath when I see my curtains erupt into flames. I scan the room and spot a candle knocked over on the floor. I must have left it burning last night and it fell during our scuffle.

"Lucy! We have to get out of here!" I shout.

I'm crawling across the floor when she catches my ankle. I kick, letting the heel of my foot land on her chin.

She still doesn't let up. She's clawing at my legs as I attempt to get to the kitchen. I need a weapon. Anything.

The fire alarms sound. Smoke fills the air around us and I cough, standing to my feet. Just as I wretch open the kitchen drawer, I feel it. The sharp sting of the knife, stabbing straight through my flesh.

CHAPTER 56

Greyson

Adam's truck skids into Tilly's driveway just as the firefighters are dousing the house with water.

I jump out, not bothering to shut the door. I rush the porch, but the fire chief cuts me off.

"Greyson, you can't go in there." He holds up his hand.

I'd known him since I was a kid, and I could tell by the look on his face it was bad.

"Is she in there?" I step to him. "I need to get to her."

He rips off his helmet. "You just missed her. Ambulance left ten minutes ago."

I tun around, motioning to Adam to get back to the truck. "Hospital," I call out.

Adam slaps his light on top of his cab and flips on the flashers as we speed through town. The hospital wasn't far, but enough time for my muscles to practically turn inside out. Tension wraps around my spine and my shoulders grow taunt.

Adam slides us right up to the automatic doors, then we're rushing inside, jogging towards the emergency room where the ambulance would have come. I stop the first nurse I see. My breathing is ragged. I could run hours on the football field, but *this shit* was different. This was *her*.

"The ambulance that just came in. From the fire. Where is she?"

Her eyes glance away then back as she flicks them down to her clip board.

"The woman they just brought in." My voice sounds harsh, but I need some answers. Now. "Where is she?"

She stutters her words. "Sssir. I'm sorry to inform you. The patient was deceased upon arrival. Her body is being prepared for transport."

What?

I stagger away, my vision blurring. "No." My back hits the wall as I suck in a deep breath.

She can't be gone. *There's no way my Rosie is gone.*

I place my hands on the back of my head.

"She's gone," I mumble.

Adam appears in front of me, his face distraught. "Grey?"

"She's...." I choke on my own sob. "They said she's...." Tears fill my eyes, then I hear it.

"Greyson?"

My head snaps in the direction of Tilly's voice.

Alive.

She's sitting in a wheelchair, her father standing behind her, along with Camille and Whitley.

"Rosie?" The word is strained. Barely slipping through my lips.

"I'm ok." She tries to stand, but Cap lays a hand on her shoulder.

I meet her midway, dropping to my knees in front of her. "They told me you didn't make it." She snakes her arms around my neck. "Fuck, I thought I'd never see you again."

She cries into the crook of my neck. She smells like smoke and her hair is coated with ashes.

Jace comes barreling around the hallway with Easton in tow as I held Tilly in my arms.

"Lucy." She sucks in a breath, then pulls back to face me. "It was Lucy."

I scrunch my brow. "What do you mean?"

"It was her. She did it all. She killed Blaine and set you up. She was in the house...she's crazy...."

"Hey." I wipe away the tears that slide down her cheeks. "It's ok. What happened? Did she hurt you?"

"It's a flesh wound. They stitched her up good," Cap answers.

"Have they arrested her?" I ask.

"No...she.... didn't make it." Tilly peers up at her father.

That must have been who the nurse was referring to.

"Why would Lucy do all of this? I thought y'all were friends?" I ask, tucking a piece of hair behind her ear.

"Let's get Tilly discharged then we'll lay it all out, Grey. We still need to get the report from Tilly." Jace slides his hands in his pockets. "It's been a long couple of days."

He was right. It *had* been a long couple of days, and I was never leaving this woman's side again.

CHAPTER 57

Tilly

"Apparently this wasn't the first time Lucy has had a run in with the law. She was arrested in Mountain Lake six years ago for stalking." Jace announces.

"I never saw it." I shift on my childhood couch, trying to get comfortable.

It's literally the same one since I was a kid. My dad had saved for months to buy the set for my mother and even though it's worn, none of us seem to be able to part with it.

I wince as I tuck my legs underneath me. Thank God the knife didn't slice all the way through. It was a deep cut, but nothing some stitches and rest couldn't fix.

"Baby, sit still. You're going to rip your stitches." Greyson scolds as he places a fresh cup of lemonade in front of me.

I thought he was overbearing before, now all he's done is hover and panic over every move I make. I'm two seconds away from sending him on a pointless errand so I can breathe.

"I'm fine Greyson." I roll my eyes.

The pain pills they gave me were doing their job, so it actually wasn't too bad.

"I knew something was off this morning." Cami slips her hand into Jace's. "You can ask him. I was up at five. Couldn't sleep."

Jace leans over and kisses her head. "She's telling the truth. I was up with her."

I glance around the room. Whitley sits at the bar, letting June paint her nails a hideous shade of yellow.

Elle has been crying ever since they got here, and poor Easton has been doing everything he can to soothe her.

"No one could have known." Jace says.

"Why didn't this come up in her background check?" I ask.

"She wasn't convicted. The person ended up dropping the charges if she agreed to psychiatric help." Jace lifts a shoulder. "Plus, she was a minor. It's something no one saw, Tilly."

I wasn't sure what was more skin crawling. The cameras, the fact I woke up to her hovering over my sleeping body, or the shrine they found in her house. The one with pictures of me plastered all over the walls.

"We didn't get the hit until right before we got the call about the fire." Adam's arm tightens around Bekka's waist. She's been sitting on his lap at the other end of the couch.

"She seemed unstable. I wish I would have known she needed help." I admit. "I agree with whoever it was before. She needed professional help."

Then Blaine would be alive. Still my ex-fiancé, but alive. Greyson wouldn't have a murder charge tied to him with a million phone calls from news outlets already, and my house wouldn't be burnt to the ground.

Sadness forms in my chest, but I let out a small smile when I see Nelson in his cage on my dad's dining room table. The firefighters were able to save him before the flames got to him.

"I was.... blindsided." I look at Greyson. "I'm sorry you had to get dragged into this."

Greyson intertwines our fingers. "I wasn't dragged into anything. You're my person, Rosie."

He brings our clasped hands to his thigh. "Speaking of blindsided, I guess I'll let y'all know before the media does." Greyson pauses. "I'm retiring."

My father's eyebrows raise. "That's a big decision. Where do you plan to be next?"

He looks at me, so much love staring right back at me. "Wherever she is."

Adam lets out a sarcastic "awe" and Bekka elbows him in the ribs.

"While we're all sharing life altering news..." Elle sniffs. "I'm pregnant."

I shriek. Immediately gripping my side when a sharp pain hits me.

"Damn it, Tilly," Greyson barks.

Cami screams and Bekka tumbles off the back of the couch. Laughter bubbles from every corner of the room and I had no idea how bad I needed it until this moment.

Someone knocks on the door, and my father stands to answer. Jordan Carmichael strides into the living room. Still in a ridiculously expensive suit and not a hair out of place.

"Look who stopped by," my father calls out.

Jordan waves a hand. "I was heading to the airport. Just wanted to shake your hand, Greyson."

Greyson stands, meeting him in the dining room. "Thanks man. I appreciate you coming all the way out here "

"Not a problem. It's my job." He moves his eyes to Jace. "It wasn't half bad getting to drink a few with my brother. It's been a while."

"You're welcome anytime, Jordan." Camille smiles.

Whitley scoffs from the bar and I eye her as she clearly pretends to not be checking out the backside of Jordan. The man isn't ugly by no means.

"I'll keep that in mind." He looks to me, then Grey. "I'm glad things worked out."

I smile at him. "Me too."

He turns to leave when I look over my shoulder. "Don't you have a flight to catch too, Whit?" I ask.

She shoots daggers at me over June's head.

"Maybe you two could carpool to the airport?" I bite my lip to keep from laughing.

Her eyes form tiny slits. "I'd rather bathe in acid. I'll pass."

Jordan checks his watch. "Your loss, cupcake." He nods towards the door. "Take care."

He leaves the room and Whitley holds up a hand. "I don't want to hear it." She rises from her barstool and stomps out to the patio.

Amused glances bounce around the room, but we all know better than to poke the bear.

Greyson sits back down on the couch, his arm sliding onto the back so my head can rest on his shoulder.

The last two weeks have been eye opening. My heart was broken, so tired, but Greyson put it back together. It wasn't that he shattered it, he was just *missing*. I couldn't fix it without my missing puzzle piece. I couldn't fix it without *him*.

CHAPTER 58

Greyson

Three months later

"Just take my hand. I thought you trusted me, Rosie?" I chuckle.

"I mean I do, but I'm blindfolded, Greyson. It's a little alarming," she mutters.

I take her hand, leading her down the rocky lake shore. It's been three months since the charges were dropped. I had announced my retirement, Tilly had recovered from her wounds, the physical ones. It's taken her some time to deal with what happened with Lucy. Tilly has always been someone who takes her friendships seriously. She loves hard. Especially her relationships she's built through the center, and it was hard for her to accept it at first. She still mourned the loss of her friend, even though she did horrible things. That's just who Tilly was.

She's not only came out of this stronger, but her confidence in her voice has grown. She still prefers to sign in loud places, but her insecurities are shrinking. I made it my personal job to make sure she knows every single day how amazing she is. How her visions for the center and this town have helped so many people.

We just left the center, where we sat down with Dixie and went over the new expansion plans to the building. I've had an idea for a while now. When I found out my career would be ending, I knew I wanted to channel my energy into something important. Something that wasn't just important to me, but to *us*. Which is why in two weeks we break ground on the new wing that is specifically devoted to kids and pre-teen athletes. We want every child that has a dream to play sports be able to interact and learn just like everyone else.

"Are we there yet? I'm starving." She groans.

"Almost." I tug, placing her right where I want her.

"Alright. We're here."

I untie the blindfold and slip it into my pocket.

"The lake?" She smiles. "What are we doing here?"

I lift a shoulder. "It's where it all began."

She faces me and purses her lips. "Is it now?"

I nod. "February 10th."

She freezes. "Ten."

I smirk, waiting for her to connect the dots.

"Greyson. Your jersey number was ten." She gasps.

"I know. That's why I chose it." I lean down and drop a kiss on the tip of her nose. "It was the day I fell in love with you, Tilly Harper."

Her cheeks flush. "That's so......sweet." She wraps her arm around my waist. "I love you "

My arms embrace her small body, as we stare out at the water. It's summertime now and the lake is clear and the trees green.

"So, what do you think about putting it right over there?" I point.

She turns. "Put what over there?"

"Our house." I untangle our arms and walk towards the spot I have marked.

"Did you just say *our* house?"

"I did." I glance back at her. "Your dad sold me this chunk of land."

"When?" She stalks towards me.

"Two years ago."

"Two years!" She squawks.

"I told you. Everything I've ever done was with you at the front of my mind, Rosie."

She smiles, so genuine. *So beautiful.*

"And I think right here would be the perfect spot where I can sit on this porch and watch you skate."

Her feet carry her across the rocks and fallen pine, and she launches herself at me. I catch her, letting her legs wrap around me.

"You're my end game, Tilly Harper. Always have been," I whisper in her ear.

She squeezes me tighter before she whispers back. "Always."

CHAPTER 59

Tilly

Five months later

I coo down at the sweet little bundle wrapped in a light blue blanket.

"Hi sweet boy," I whisper.

I'm holding Jasper Grey Roy in my arms as Greyson peers over my shoulder.

He may have been a professional football player, but one little whimper from his nephew has him a scrambling mess.

"He's handsome, isn't he?" I ask.

"He gets it from me." Greyson winks.

I laugh and stand to walk him back over to Easton, who's currently watching Elle scarf down a chicken leg.

"That was incredible." Easton gazes at Elle like she hung the moon herself. The stars too.

"The chicken or the baby?" Grey asks.

Easton gives him a pointed look just as Cami and Jace come in with Adam and Bekka on their heels. "We brought snacks!" Bekka chimes.

"Thank God!" Elle says through a mouth full of chicken. "I'm starving."

"You just grew a human and pushed him out of your vagiiiiii.... oh, hi June!" Bekka smooths over the inappropriate comment with a smile.

June beams from Easton's side. "I have a baby brother and he drinks from my mama's nipples."

Elle spews chicken across the room and Easton barks out a laugh.

"She's not wrong." He shrugs.

"Anyone need anything? I'm going to run down to the cafeteria. You need some ice cream, June?" I ask.

"Yes please!" She smiles wide.

I slip out of the room, letting Bekka and Cami have their turn. We've been on pins and needles since she went into labor last night.

I round the corner to see Whitley standing in the hall. *Alone.* She's here for Christmas, which is in three days. Santa came early and we all got the best present in little Jasper.

"Hey Whit," I call out.

She glances over at me. "Hey, Tills."

I step up beside her and turn to see what has my hard ass sister looking all sappy. She's gazing through the nursery window. Five little angels lay snuggled in their bassinets. I peek at her from the corner of my eye and see a look on her face I've never seen before. *Doubt.*

Whitley had always been so fierce. So sure of herself.

"What's going on Whit?" I ask. "Talk to me."

She keeps her eyes on the glass. "I'm moving back."

My heart leaps inside my chest. I've waited almost ten years to hear those words.

"You are?" I face her.

She faces me, her eyes growing misty. "I am."

I wrap her in a hug, so thankful that *all* of my family will be together again. In Timber Creek.

She squeezes me tight before her broken voice whispers. "Tilly, I'm pregnant."

The end....

Afterword

Thank you for reading Shadows of Timber Creek! I hope you enjoyed these characters as much as I enjoyed writing them!
Curious about the oldest Harper sister?
Whitley and Jordan's story
Wreckage of Timber Creek is a single mom, boss/workplace, enemies to lovers, romantic suspense!
The final book of the Timber Creek Series

COMING SOON!

For information on future release dates be sure to sign up for my newsletter or follow me on social media

http://www.authorsjchaynie.com

Acknowledgements

First and foremost, I want to thank the readers! Without you I wouldn't even be writing these books. A huge shoutout to my family and friends who stuck by me through this entire process. This was my most challenging book to date. I really wanted to make the story perfect, while also being as authentic as I could with some delicate topics. A person that was a huge inspiration for this book is my cousin, Callie. She inspired the character of Tilly Harper, and she continues to amaze me every day. I'm so thankful to have so many people in my corner. From my beta readers to those who help edit, to my ARC readers and street team. You are not taken for granted and I am truly grateful to each one of you!

ABOUT THE AUTHOR

S.J. Chaynie is a small-town Texas girl who has found a love for writing. She enjoys writing romance, with a sprinkle of suspense, and a little humor. If she is not busy writing her newest ideas, she is spending time with her husband and two beautiful daughters. She believes a good book and a lot of laughs is the best medicine. She brings suspense, love, angst, and sometimes the occasional heartbreak to her stories. Always a HEA, but every character and story she holds close to her heart and hopes they touch yours as well.

www.ingramcontent.com/pod-product-compliance
Lightning Source LLC
Chambersburg PA
CBHW051144130726
47988CB00005B/1983